Blind Buddy
and
Mojo's Blues Band

BLIND BUDDY
AND
MOJO'S BLUES BAND

by

NAN MAHON

iUniverse, Inc.
New York Bloomington

Blind Buddy and Mojo's Blues Band

iUniverse books may be ordered through booksellers or by contacting:

iUniverse
1663 Liberty Drive
Bloomington, IN 47403
www.iuniverse.com
1-800-Authors (1-800-288-4677)

ISBN: 978-1-4502-2081-1 (pbk)
ISBN: 978-1-4502-2082-8 (ebook)

Printed in the United States of America

iUniverse rev. date: 4/23/10

Dedicated to the late Mac McAuley
"Big Mac Daddy"
Blues club owner

For all the good times at the round table in
The Brewery where his friends
gathered to hear the music he loved.

Chapter One

Saturday night and a full moon can be a menacing combination at any night spot on the low side of town where folks are throwing off the restrictions of a hard work week and partying without boundaries. Such a place was Aunt Martha's Blues and Barbecue Shack where the crowd filled every seat, stood two deep at the bar, and lined the walls. All the elements for trouble echoed in the rumble of voices and raucous music that rose up and reverberated out into the night.

In the days before World War II, they would have called a place like Aunt Martha's a juke joint. Today, it is an unpainted plank building on the edge of Memphis frequented by working class black folks and white blues lovers. None of the chairs matched and some of the tables were discards from people's houses. In the old days they sold bootleg liquor in jelly jars. Now, the bar offered only beer and wine. But there was a kitchen that served barbecue smothered with a spicy red sauce and chunky home fries ordered through a square cut in the interior wall. Pork ribs, catfish and chicken were cooked out behind the building on an oil drum cut in half and filled with hickory chips. Its smoke bellowed gray against the dark night and a rich aroma filled the air.

A jump blues tune went on, blasting out the door propped open with a chair wedged against the knob, providing breathing air and cooling relief for the sweating bodies on the dance floor. The beat could be felt in the hard-pack dirt parking lot where whiskey was drunk from bottles tipped up and passed around; where murky deals involving drugs and contraband went down; and couples had sex in cars because waiting until they got home seemed unreasonable and not nearly as exciting.

The place wasn't owned by anybody's Aunt Martha, but by a short, chubby black man named Jake Washington who wore multiple diamond rings on his fingers and carried rolls of hundred dollar bills in the bib pocket of his overalls. He was a shrewd and successful man who preyed on his own people; a slum lord who dabbled in numbers, drugs and prostitution. He moved in a dangerous world.

In this world, on this Saturday night, Blind Buddy and Mojo's Blues Band took the stage at Aunt Martha's Blues and Barbecue Shack.

Mojo's Blues Band was playing jump blues, the kind that packs the floor with couples moving in complete freedom, burning up energy and laughing as they dance. Aunt Martha's dark, smoke-filled club had a stage so small the quintet stood close enough to touch each other.

The group's leader, Buddy O'Brian, played a scarred-up old Gibson with such creativity that his riffs took the breath away from aspiring guitarists and veterans alike. Seeing the world through a series of lines, shadows and dark images, Buddy seemed to become one with the instrument in his hands, so that people wondered if there was magic in his darkness.

At Buddy's feet lay Mojo, a black and tan German Shepard, eighty pounds of muscle and mean. The harness on his shoulders identified him as a Seeing Eye dog.

When the song ended, exhausted dancers ebbed from the floor, leaning on each other and laughing. The band began a sultry, sun-going-down kind of music as their singer, Nina, stumbled up the two shaky steps and across the stage to the microphone just in front of Buddy.

He felt the unsteadiness of her walk, made out her shadowy form in the long, tight dress as she staggered and caught herself from falling sideways. It was her second set of the evening and Buddy remembered she had been fine during the first one. She must have gotten high on something during the break.

All her talk about being clean and staying that way, Buddy thought, was gone now.

Buddy remembered the days when he had been riding the cocaine cloud, and the sweet distance it put between him and the world. Clean for five years now, the yearning for it still came back sometimes, but not as often as it used to. Even then it was the oblivion that a bottle of Jack Daniels gave him that Buddy preferred. Sometimes, even today, he had to seek that escape again, to fill the hole in his soul. A few years back, his song *Trying to Cry You Back Home*, had been number on one the charts. But when he slipped into the dark world of drugs, music had taken a backseat to getting high and he hadn't had a hit song since. At thirty-one, he was still playing places like Aunt Martha's.

He leaned over to Strum, the bass guitar player standing next to him, "She's loaded."

"Yeah," came the sarcastic reply, "she's better that way."

The keyboard opened the song and Nina began to sing. There was sadness in her voice as she crooned a low, emotional song that said she missed her man, her hometown and all that had once made her happy. Couples on the floor swayed in place, holding onto each other, catching their breath and cooling down. Bodies against bodies, hands slid along the curve of a hip or traveled across the skin of a bare shoulder. Lips touched and unspoken promises were made.

Buddy listened as Nina hesitated in her phrases as if she had forgotten the lyrics and then threw in words of her own, going off key more than once.

Franklin, at the key board, played half sitting, half standing, his blond hair in a long ponytail bouncing as he moved in rhythm. Buddy recognized Franklin was trying to cover for Nina, filling in gaps in the song, doing some creative things on the keyboard to make up for her lapse in the words. The ivories rang under his fingers, creating a low-down blues style that echoed the pain in Nina's voice.

In the middle of the chorus, Nina stumbled backward, catching herself just before she went down. Amos, the second-lead guitarist, had moved so that he was standing next to her. Pulling the guitar strap from around his neck, he laid the instrument on the floor and put his arm around Nina to lead her off stage.

She's through, Buddy thought, never missing a beat in spite of the anger rushing up in him. I won't put up with this shit.

Buddy reached out to find the microphone and continued the song where Nina's voice had faded away. He sang in his low, raspy style, and Mojo, leaning against Buddy's leg, raised his head to listen and then settled back onto his forelegs to sleep.

The band went back to the jump tunes, played some roadhouse blues, and kept the walls ringing and the crowd wild. Strum worked with a slouch hat pulled low on his forehead and never looked up from his guitar. Rufus, the drummer, pushed the music forward with a steady beat. He was a big man with dark blue-black skin that glistened with perspiration as he worked. There was a red bandana tied around his forehead to keep the sweat that streamed down his face from running into his eyes.

Amos came back on stage and picked up his guitar. He was a handsome man with light chocolate skin and a brilliant smile. He rocked with every note he played, moving from one foot to the other in perpetual motion.

When there was a pause in the music, a bell rang, its brass sound carrying across the room.

"Last call!"

Buddy leaned into the microphone, "I'm Buddy O'Brian with Mojo's Blues Band. I want to thank ya'll for coming out tonight. Hope ya'll all had a good time and we'll see ya'll next time we're in Memphis."

The band went into their theme song, *Trying to Cry You Back Home*. People were leaving the floor, making a last pitch to dance partners to spend the rest of the night with them, draining the last drops of beer from warm bottles, gathering their things and straggling out the door. Most dropped a dollar or two in the tip jar as they went by; yelling to the band, telling them it was a hella night.

Buddy was slipping his guitar into its soft traveling case when he heard the quick steps of someone running across the room.

"Call the cops!" a man yelled.

Must be a knife fight in the parking lot, Buddy thought. It was a Saturday night ritual; someone had someone else's woman, or insulted someone's date. Fists, broken beer bottles and knives were the weapons of choice as men, and sometimes women, went at each other between parked cars. Tomorrow they would nurse black eyes, bruises and cuts, bragging about how they took the other guy out. Usually the loser did most of the boasting.

Buddy was sitting on the stage with Mojo, waiting for Rufus to finish disassembling his drums and haul them to the van just outside the door, when a step creaked on the stairs. Mojo didn't move as the shadow approached Buddy.

"What?"

"It's Nina," Franklin said. "What'd you want me to do?"

"See if you can get her to the motel, will you? I'll talk to her tomorrow."

"Okay." Franklin started to move away but Buddy grabbed his arm.

"What's the problem in the parking lot?"

Sirens were coming closer as police cars rolled onto the dirt lot, screeching to a stop.

"I donno, but the bartender's running across the room." Franklin raised his voice, "Raymond, what happened?"

"Jake Washington, the owner. He's been stabbed. Think he's dead."

Chapter Two

Mojo growled deep in his throat as footsteps came near and stopped in front of Buddy.

"What's the matter with him?" a man asked.

"You're too close." Buddy patted the dog's head.

"You the one called Blind Buddy?"

"Yeah." Buddy shook his head. "Never could figure that out."

A chuckle from the man, then, "I'm Detective John Allen, Shelby County Sheriff's Department. "Can I see some ID?"

"Left my driver's license home, but here's a photo ID." Buddy handed his wallet over to the officer who smiled at the dry humor.

"Your name James Patrick O'Brian, Jr.?"

"Means there's two of us, so they call me Buddy."

"Address is in Baton Rouge." Detective Allen gave the wallet back, pressing it against Buddy's hand.

"We're on tour. Going home tomorrow." Buddy stuffed the wallet inside his back pocket. "Been on the road a couple of months now."

"You out in the parking lot anytime tonight?"

"Nope. Dangerous out there."

"How 'bout your band members?"

"Have to ask them."

"You know Jake Washington?"

"Some. Hear someone did him in tonight."

"Stuck an ice pick in his ear while he was sitting in his Cadillac."

Buddy said nothing, thinking of Jake with an ice pick in his head, bleeding on the soft leather interior of his El Dorado.

"Old Jake was a mean son-of-a-bitch, but that's still a hard way to go," mused the detective. "Got any idea who would do something like that?"

"Can't say I do."

"I'll talk to your band members." Mojo growled again as the detective started to leave, and then turned back.

"You the guy had that big hit a few years back? What's it called, *Crying You Back* or something like that?"

"*Trying to Cry You Back Home.*"

"Man, I love that song. Bought the CD. Almost wore it out."

Buddy put out his hand. "Thanks. If I can think of anything, I'll let you know. We'd like to get to bed now."

"Sure. Go on. We'll catch up with you if we need you."

"Okay if my guys go too? I'm the designated driver, you know."

The detective was laughing as he walked away. Then Strum came up and asked, "You ready to go?"

Buddy put his hand on Strum's arm and they started toward the back door of Aunt Martha's.

"Damn Strum, they put an ice pick in his ear. Even Jake wasn't rotten enough to deserve that."

Chapter Three

Buddy sat at the table of the motor home, a mug of coffee in front of him and his guitar beside him. His chambray shirt was hanging loose over faded jeans and he wore penny loafers without socks. His dark hair curled just above the gold loop in his right ear.

"I think we're going to have to replace Nina," he said.

"Singers are a dime a dozen," Strum mumbled from beneath the hat tilted over his eyes. He was riding in the shotgun seat while Franklin sat behind the wheel of the Winnebago, driving with the Sunday afternoon traffic as a light rain began tapping against the windshield. Amos slept, snoring occasionally, while stretched out on the bed at the rear of the coach. After two months on the road, they were heading home.

"Not like Nina, though," Franklin did a half turn in his seat, "she's the best."

"I believe you got a case of the hots for that little sweet piece of chocolate," Strum said. "What makes you think she'd mess with a cracker kid like you?"

"She can stay with the band or not. It's up to her," Buddy said. "I had a talk with her, told her I wouldn't put up with her showing up on stage loaded and stumbling around. She keeps using, she has to go."

He felt bad about that. When she was clean, Nina was a powerful singer, putting everything she had into a song. She cried when he told her that if she didn't get clean, he'd have to let her go. She promised him she'd kick the cocaine, said she wasn't really hooked. But he'd been there; he knew the stranglehold signs of addiction.

Franklin shoved a blues CD in the dash player and the high twang of a guitar filled the motor home. Buddy fingered the strings on his Gibson.

"I hope Eldon doesn't have us booked for a week or two, I could use some time off," he said.

"I'm with you, man," Franklin said. "I can get in a carpenter job or two with my dad and make some money. Maybe get my union card this time."

"Boy, are you a carpenter or a musician?" Strum demanded. "Reminds me, though, Buddy, you think Eldon got our money before they wasted old Jake."

"He gets it before the gig." Buddy slid his palm down the guitar strings. "Musicians get the short end too often. Gotta get the money up front."

They were silent for a while; a low-down blues song coming over the speakers.

"Who you think did Jake?" asked Franklin.

"Could've been lots of people." Buddy tightened the third string and tested the sound. "Old Jake was the devil himself."

"Never heard of anybody stickin' an ice pick in somebody's ear," Franklin said. "Don't know anybody who'd do something like that. Why'd they just shoot him?"

"Got what he had comin', you ask me," Strum said. "Any bologna left in the fridge? I'm hungry."

"Can you make me a sandwich too? And a Dr. Pepper?" Franklin asked, adding "'Cause I'm driving."

"You want one, Buddy?" Strum offered.

"Not now, just a Dr. Pepper. Try not to wake up Amos. I don't think he got any sleep last night."

"He didn't come back to the room at all," said Franklin, who roomed with Amos when they were on the road. "Must have got lucky."

"Ever know him not to?" Strum said.

They traveled on along the rain soaked highway lined with dogwood blossoms and trees bending in the wind, leaving Tennessee behind and moving through Mississippi toward Louisiana and home. In Mississippi, live oak trees were spun with Spanish moss, hanging like giant spider webs reaching almost to the ground. The late spring day began to fade as they made the change of highways and grew closer to the Louisiana line.

"Can you see Rufus and Nina behind us?" Buddy asked.

"Yeah, the van's a couple of cars back," Franklin answered.

Buddy thought of a petulant Nina riding beside Rufus in the van carrying the drums and sound equipment. Rufus usually drove the Winnebago, but he said he would drive the van and see if he could straighten Nina out. Buddy hoped Rufus could talk some sense into her, maybe calm her down.

"I hope my momma got some chicken and dumplings cooked up," said Franklin. "And a big pan of cornbread."

"Boy, you too old to be stayin' with you momma and daddy," Strum admonished, turning sideways in his seat to face the driver. "What are you, twenty-four now?"

"I like it there with everybody. My brothers and I play basketball in the backyard and touch football in the park. I like going to work with my daddy too." Franklin switched on the headlights as the sky grew dimmer. "What're you gonna do when we get home?"

"Just hang with my woman." Strum smiled, leaned back and crossed his arms on his chest.

"Don't know why a fine woman like Ruthie puts up with your sorry ass." Buddy was sitting sideways, his feet up on the bench-seat. "She works all the time at that hospital and comes home to wait on you."

"She knows a good man when she sees one." Strum pushed the hat back on his head and pulled a CD from the dash and pushed in a new one. John Lee Hooker came on with an old, front porch kind of blues and a voice that barely made the scales.

"She's blinder than I am," Buddy said.

"Now that our boy gone out on his own, well hey, I'm all she got," Strum said from under his hat.

"Louisiana state line just up ahead," Franklin called out. "Almost home."

Everyone grew quiet, the lights of Baton Rouge flashing in the night as they drove on; drawing closer to it and the people they loved. Music from the CD player filled the silence; some blues band heavy with guitars and a harmonica taking the lead. Buddy was lost in his own private thoughts, thinking of what he missed most on the long, lonely days on the road. He thought of Ivy and the silk of her hair as it fell across his face when she kissed him. He remembered the easiness of home, of knowing every inch of the space he shared with the woman he loved and had loved since they were kids.

It was midnight when Franklin left Buddy and Mojo at the door of their condo; Franklin standing there until Buddy fitted the key in the lock and stepped in, closing the door behind him. Just inside the entry, Buddy put down his duffle bag and slipped the soft guitar case from his shoulder. The warm feeling of home rushed at him, the sweet familiarity and perfume of it surrounding him. Mojo became restless, moving around, straining at the leash.

"Buddy?" Ivy's voice called.

Mojo whined and pulled at the restraint, so that Buddy unhooked the leash and released him. "All right, go on to her."

He heard the dog running across the floor and Ivy speaking to him.

"Good boy," she crooned. "I'm glad you're home."

Buddy knew she was rubbing the fur on Mojo's neck, kissing the top of his wet nose, while the dog whined and lapped at her with his tongue.

Then she was there with her arms around Buddy, her face against his, her lips whispering how she missed him, how glad she was he was home. He slipped his arms inside the open satin robe she wore and held her body to him. It was warm and slender, just as it has been in his thoughts all the way from Memphis.

"Sorry we woke you up darlin'," he mumbled as he nuzzled her neck.

"Seems like you've been gone so long," she said.

A gardenia fragrance surrounded her as it always did, and her long hair brushed against his face, just as it did in his dreams. He knew it was light brown, the kind of hair that bleached almost colorless in the summer sun. As kids they had swam in the community pool and her skin had tanned to a golden brown, while her hair grew lighter. Back in the days when he could see her face, look into her hazel eyes.

She pulled back a little, still holding his face in her hands, her long fingers spread on his cheeks. "You hungry?"

"Maybe a little."

"Sit down, I'll make a sandwich. Got some pastrami, is that alright?"

"Anything," he said.

He walked to the living room, remembering every step, every object along the way. Touching the sofa, he felt the seat cushion and sat down. Ivy had told him the sofa was poppy red with white throw pillows and the big chair nearby was white with red pillows. He remembered red; sometimes he pictured it in his mind, the brightness and the authority of it. When he played his guitar, many of the riffs he created were red, like flames against the rhythm section beating steady behind him. Red was also the color of blood, the kind that must have been on the white leather upholstery of Jake Washington's Cadillac after someone put an ice pick in his ear.

Buddy settled against the sofa cushion and kicked off his loafers, working his toes in the thick carpet. It was one of those things he could do at home that he never did anywhere else. Music came into the room;

low so it did not intrude. Ivy always had the radio in the bedroom tuned to a jazz station. They were playing a June Christy CD. He knew Christy was Ivy's favorite singer.

Ivy set a plate with a sandwich on the coffee table and took his hand in hers. She placed his fingers on the food so he would know where it was.

"Welcome home," she said.

Settling on the sofa, she pulled her feet up underneath her and he could feel her leaning against him. Ever since they were in elementary school she had been his best friend, the one who begged him not to run with the street gang, the one who sat beside his hospital bed and held his hand when they told him the blow from the swinging chain of a rival gang member took ninety percent of his sight, and she was the one who stayed with him when the world moved into dark shadows.

"Ivy, I've got some new songs and I want to make an album." He drank from the glass filled with cola she gave him. "Will you sing for me?"

"Nina's your singer."

"She's using again."

Ivy sat up, moving away from him. "I'm a jazz singer, Buddy."

"Blues is just a poor man's jazz." He reached for the sandwich and bit into it.

"Oh, I could do something like Diana Washington or Etta James, I guess." Ivy moved back against him. "But I don't have the range or volume for anything too gritty. We've talked about this before."

"Billie Holiday was really a blues singer, you know," he said. "She just crossed over to jazz. You realize she had no range at all."

He thought of Ivy when they were sixteen, with her sitting beside him on the piano bench while he played and she sang some Billie Holiday song she loved, like *Good Morning Heartache*. Her voice was throaty and expressive, capable of reaching for the emotional depth and intimacy that made a jazz song unique. Now, she sang in supper clubs on weekends. Maybe she could have made a name for herself, but she refused to leave Baton Rouge to go on tour because, she argued, he might need her. Weekdays, she worked as a casualty adjuster for a large multi-line insurance company.

"I just need you for this session. A few low key numbers," he drained the glass and put it on the table, "written with you in mind."

She leaned over and kissed the side of his face where an old scar made a thin line from his eyebrow to his cheekbone. "You know I'll do anything you want me to. I'm so glad you're home."

Pulling her into his lap, he whispered, "You're the reason I come back to this town. You're my home."

He picked her up and carried her into the bedroom and the rumpled, familiar bed.

Chapter Four

Buddy slept late the next morning. He woke to the urgent nudge of Mojo's cold nose and low whine. Picking yesterday's jeans up from the floor, he pulled them on and stumbled across the room to open the sliding door to let the dog out onto the fenced patio. He made his way to the kitchen and pushed the coffee on button, knowing that Ivy would have set it up before she left for work. In a moment there was the familiar sound of dripping and the fresh coffee aroma. When the phone rang, he walked across the room to the desk and felt for the receiver.

"Mr. O'Brian?"

"That's right."

"This is Gary at the storage yard where you keep your Winnebago."

"Yeah? We brought it in last night around midnight."

"I'm sorry to tell you, someone broke into it. Vandalized it pretty bad."

"Damn! Don't you have security there?"

"Security found it this morning. We called the police already. Need you to come down and sign the papers, take a look and see what's missing." There was a silence, then, "Sorry."

Buddy was used to people being embarrassed when they used the wrong words. "I'll be there in a while."

He disconnected then punched the speed dial. When his band manager picked up, Buddy said, "Eldon, I need you to come and take me to the storage. Someone broke into my RV and trashed it."

Eldon Dubois had the lazy kind of southern drawl that made Buddy want to reach down his throat and pull the words out. Other people got impatient on a regular basis and finished Eldon's sentences for him.

"Well hey, Buddy," he drawled, "I was meaning to call you this morning, make sure ya'll got back alright. I heard about ole Jake getting' taken out couple nights ago. That was the night ya'll were playing there wasn't it?"

"That's right. Someone poked an ice pick in his ear."

"Never heard of anyone doin' that before," Eldon drawled. "Musta cheated the wrong person. Well, my daddy always said if you lay down with dogs you get fleas, or in this case, dead."

"He was bad company alright," Buddy agreed, tired of the conversation.

"Good news is I got paid up front," Eldon said. "Got a check for you."

"Just bring it when you come." Buddy hung up.

He took a shower, put the same jeans back on and found a fresh polo shirt in his dresser drawer. It was an hour later that Eldon knocked on the door. Mojo growled low in his throat as Eldon came in, pushing past Buddy and entering the room as if it belonged to him.

"That dog never liked me," Eldon said.

"And you're so damn likable too," Buddy said.

Buddy knew Eldon was a tall, white man who always wore a suit and tie with custom made dress shirts in assorted colors. The band members called Eldon a fancy man and laughed at his slick ways, making fun of the high shine on his shoes and the wide smile on his lips. The musicians didn't trust Eldon, but he was good at what he did and kept the band working even during the slow times. Lately, Buddy was feeling his band was worth more and could be booked into better places than Aunt Martha's.

Eldon put an envelope in Buddy's hand. "Here's your money. Told the others they would have to come to my office for theirs."

Buddy took the envelope and placed it in a large dish near the door where mail accumulated. "Ivy'll take care of it. I want to talk to you about cutting a new CD. Set me up with a studio and crew."

"You got enough new stuff?"

"I wrote some songs and we can add some covers." Buddy turned in Eldon's direction. "We can start rehearsing right away. Ivy'll sing three songs and I'll do the others."

Eldon didn't hide the surprise in his voice, "No Nina? Is there—"

Buddy cut him off. "Going to let her go. She's a practicing junkie and I don't want her on stage loaded."

"When'd all this happen?"

"She was trouble all through the tour. I decided she had to go when she almost passed out on stage in Memphis."

Buddy ran his hands over the slashed upholstery of his motor home. The mattress was pulled from the bed and torn open. Everything was emptied from the cabinets and closet; clothes and dishes covered the narrow floor.

"Shit!" He shouted and punched the wall, rocking the vehicle.

"Yeah, it's pretty bad," the security man said. "Know how you must feel. I'd be pissed too."

"Is there spray paint anywhere?"

"No. Most times, when this happens, people are looking for something," the guard said from the doorway. "Usually money or guns."

"Never keep nothing like that in here," Buddy said. "They just wasted their time."

"How about drugs?"

Buddy stepped out of the vehicle. He could make out the shadow of the ground and used his cane to judge the distance.

"You ask that of everyone or just musicians?" Already on edge, Buddy's temper was rising.

"Just asking." The guard's voice was apologetic. "Because, you know they didn't seem to take anything. Stereo is still there with the CDs and there's a guitar."

"Just not musical, I guess."

"Say you brought it in after midnight?"

"Yeah. Came off tour, drove in from Memphis."

"Saw where a guy was murdered there last night at some blues club. That where you were?"

"Matter of fact, it was." Buddy closed the Winnebago door.

"Some of those places—those joints," said the guard, "well, they're just bad news."

"Give me the damn papers to sign and I'll call my insurance company." Buddy snapped his fingers and Mojo came to his side.

"Funny thing though," the guard said, "they didn't bother any of the other vehicles besides yours. Usually, they break into a bunch of them."

"You think they targeted mine for some reason?"

"I'm just sayin'."

Back in the car, Buddy knew he didn't want to be with Eldon and he didn't want to be alone because the need for the dark magic of Jack Daniels

Black Label was crawling up his spine. His anger over the break-in was still seething beneath the surface.

"Eldon, you can drop me off in Spanish Town. I wanna talk to my dad."

Eldon drove across Baton Rogue to the old district where history lived on every corner and faded memories of Spanish rule were part of the fabric. On the far edge, where time and progress had moved on and left buildings and streets in decay were the pockmarks of what had been the color and flavor of the Old South.

"Here we are, Jimmy O'Brian's Irish Pub," Eldon sneered.

"Jes' let me off in front," Buddy said as Eldon pulled to the curb. "Mojo'll take me on in."

"How you gettin' home?"

"I'll be okay. Thanks for the lift." Buddy opened the car door and stepped to the sidewalk. Mojo leaped over the seat and stood near him.

Buddy took the leash and rubbed the dog's head. "You know where we are, don't you boy?"

Inside the bar was cool and dark. A front-porch blues song by some forgotten legend played low on the jukebox; otherwise it was quiet in the mid-afternoon. Business was not good, Buddy knew, as he walked to the bar.

Every inch of this place was burned into his memory and it popped up in his mind like a picture. The bar was long with a mirror in back and rows of liquor bottles on selves in front. A popcorn machine, always half full of stale popcorn sat at one end and an antiquated cash register still rang up bar tabs.

Buddy leaned against the bar's cool surface. "Plain Seven-up with a little lemon squeeze."

"Saints be praised!" a big Irish voice boomed. "It's our Buddy home again."

Jimmy O'Brian leaned across the bar and grabbed both of Buddy's arms. "The wee people have brought you home safe."

Mojo gave a protective bark and Buddy pulled away from his father's grip. "How are you, Jimmy?"

"I'm fine, my boy. It's a cool drink you'll be needing now."

Buddy settled on a stool while Mojo lay on the worn hardwood floor. Jimmy sang a little Irish jingle and Buddy heard him pull the tab from a can of Seven-up and pour it into a beer mug. The aroma of cabbage cooking came from the back room.

"Business not so good, Jimmy?"

"We're keeping the doors open." Jimmy put the glass in Buddy's hand. "It's not as lively here as when we had your dear mother, saints rest her soul."

Jimmy swiped a towel across the bar, the damp cloth running up against Buddy's hand. "Are you hungry now, boy? I've got corn beef and cabbage on the stove."

Buddy smiled, hearing the old lilt in his father's voice. "Yeah, I'll have some. I can smell it from here."

The bar gate creaked open and Jimmy's footsteps started across the room.

"Is the piano still where it was?" Buddy asked.

"Same as the last time you sat there."

Buddy made his way across the room to the piano, Mojo walking beside him. Setting on the bench, Buddy lifted the cover and ran his fingers across the keys, finding the ivory missing from two of them and the notes flat beneath his touch.

"Needs tuning, Jimmy."

"It always has, lad, even when you were making it ring so the angels themselves were listening," Jimmy called from the back room.

Buddy knew someone had entered the bar. There was a light step and then a hand on his shoulder. The air was filled with the sent of gardenia.

"Sit here beside me Ivy," he said, moving over on the bench. "Jimmy, can you bring another plate?"

Chapter Five

Buddy's mother, Yvette, was a dark eyed, light-skinned Creole girl straight from the Louisiana bayou country. When she was eighteen she went to visit her cousin in Baton Rouge. At a Saturday night dance in a little juke joint on the outskirts of town, she meet Jimmy O'Brian, a laughing Irish boy making his way through America on a lark and a shoestring. His gift of gab and his way with an Irish ballad had got him from New York to Baton Rouge.

Jimmy never went home to Ireland and Yvette stayed in Baton Rouge. The two were married within a month of meeting each other. He found a job as a singing bartender in a place similar to the one where they had met. Every night, Yvette came to the club where her buoyant manner and laughter drew people around her and men vied for the privilege to buy her drinks. Jimmy intervened when they asked for more.

Life was one continuous song and dance for the couple who lived for the free, gay nights in Baton Rogue. They made love in the small hours of morning and slept through the day's sultry heat. After Buddy was born, they scraped together enough money to buy the bar where Jimmy worked and moved into the back, living among stacks of liquor boxes and the stale smell of beer.

Buddy grew up with the bar as his playground, the regulars were his friends. Always in the middle of the action, Saturday nights would find the child asleep in the corner of the bar as the party went on.

Every night, people from the neighborhood came to listen to Jimmy singing Irish ballads as he mixed drinks. On weekends, blues or Dixieland bands would set up in the far corner and play. Patrons would dance where they could. Yvette would whirl alone across the room, lost in complete abandon, her black hair and loop earrings swinging with her movements.

By the end of the night, Jimmy would have to carry Yvette from the table where she had passed out from too many drinks of gin, to her bed in the back apartment.

At age five, Buddy crawled upon the bench of the bar's battered upright piano and started picking out by ear the songs he had heard on Saturday night. As soon as his feet could touch the piano peddles he was pounding out Stride, and by age ten, he could do the boogie and rhythm and blues. Customers cheered and threw dollars in the tip jar on top of the piano.

When the three O'Brians went to visit Yvette's relatives in the bayou country, Buddy joined the Cajun band that always appeared to play on the back porch while the family ate gumbo and drank home-made moonshine. There was Uncle Willie with an old fiddle that he held as if it was his true love; and Yvette's brother Jock with the rub strapped over his shoulders, its silver metal gleaming in the light. Jock's hands, holding the spoons, danced up and down the rub in rhythm as people called out a Cajun yell. Pierre would sing in a language that was mostly French as dancers moved in the way they had learned as children. When they let Buddy roll the old upright piano out to play beside them, he felt as if he were at heaven's gate, keeping up the Cajun rhythm they laid down.

Yvette and Jimmy danced until the last lantern light was dimmed and the musicians packed their instruments away. Jimmy and Yvette would stumble off to somewhere among the trees laden with Spanish moss, and a relative would take Buddy to a pallet where children slept.

Yvette's drinking increased until there was always the taste of gin in her kiss and the smell of it on her breath. As time went on, Jimmy was carrying Yvette to her bed more and more often, even when the afternoon sun was shining across the barroom floor. Still, to Buddy, she was a vision of beauty that whirled in a flash of bright colors and whispered adoring words to him in French.

The arguments between Jimmy and Yvette began as her drinking increased.

"Now it's a morning drink, is it?" Jimmy would say.

"Just a little eye-opener."

"You'll be three sheets to the wind by noon."

"I'm just having fun, Jimmy. You use to have fun with me."

"You've got to slow down, woman," Jimmy said. "You'll kill yourself and what will the boy do then?"

When Buddy was fifteen, Yvette died from the alcohol that poisoned and wasted her body. Jimmy insisted on holding an Irish wake in the bar where Yvette had laughed and danced. Candles burned on every surface and in every corner of the shadowy room as old friends and Yvette's family came to say good-bye. Platters of food were laid out along the bar and soulful Irish music gave background to whispered regrets and condolences.

Buddy hated the people who came to shake their heads over his mother's body and mutter "what a shame, she was so beautiful," or "she simply drank herself to death, and "Jimmy is just devastated."

He resented the sympathetic hugs from women and pats on his shoulder from men. He wanted to shout, "Leave us alone. You didn't know her!"

Buddy looked at the cold, motionless woman lying in the casket and thought she barely resembled his mother. He could not cry for this still, lifeless thing looked only faintly like the woman he loved so much. But there was the thick black hair falling onto her shoulders and the strands of bright beads around her neck. In her ears were the large gold loops that swung as she danced, and behind them, in a second piercing, were small loops. Buddy reached over and took one of the small loops from her ear and pressed it in the palm of his hand.

Later that night, in Buddy's bedroom, Ivy rubbed alcohol on Buddy's right earlobe and stuck a needle through it into a piece of cork. She pushed Yvette's gold loop through the hole after the needle and wiped away the drops of blood.

"She's always with you now," Ivy said. "As long as you want her to be."

The joy left Jimmy O'Brian and his Irish Pub. Depression consumed Jimmy and grief was visible in his every tired movement. His carefree manner became quarrelsome and he withdrew into himself and away from Buddy.

Jimmy was a man who would buy anyone a drink, but did not tolerate someone trying to steal from him. His bulk and his Irish temper had made many men back away from a tangle with Jimmy. Now dark moods came often and he sang more sad Irish ballads than playful jigs while anger came as sudden as lightening. Without Yvette's laughter and dancing, customers began to drift away. Saturday nights were no longer filled with music. When the old customers urged Buddy to play the piano, he would run from the bar, out onto the city streets where he stayed until closing. He joined other boys there, spending the night hours on street corners and doorways gambling or smoking marijuana.

Buddy started to run with a neighborhood gang called The Lords. He was sixteen the Saturday night when he lost most of his sight in a rumble, taking the blow of a chain upside his head. It was a warm spring night, rich with humidity and a sky peppered with stars. Buddy carried a switchblade knife in the pocket of his jacket with The Lords stitched in red across the back. He walked with a swagger beside ten other boys wearing jackets like his, on their way to a rumble with the Vipers. They were high on marijuana; full of life and of themselves.

They met the Vipers in the park, near the baseball diamond where they had played as Little Leaguers not so long ago. The grass was slightly damp and smelled freshly mowed. The clash of boys began as they rushed at each other, adrenaline pumping, fists and weapons flying. There were cries of pain and curses of anger; the stars whirled in the sky and, somewhere in the distance, came the whine of sirens. Buddy didn't remember the blow that brought him down.

When he woke, he was in a hospital bed. Ivy was holding his hand and Jimmy was pleading for the wee people and all the saints to look after his son. The doctors said Buddy would be left with a vision of bright lights and shadows.

Chapter Six

Buddy worked out a phrase on the Gibson, modified it and then tried again. He liked it now, so he played it once more, his lips moving with the lyrics he was putting to it. Sitting on the floor, his back to the sofa and the guitar in his arms, he was immersed in music. Beside him, Mojo began to bark before the knock sounded on the door.

"Dammit!" Buddy, clad in a pair of faded jeans, without a shirt or shoes, stood up, still holding the guitar, and followed Mojo across the room.

"Yeah?" he said through the door.

"Detective John Allen, Shelby County Sheriff's Department," a voice said on the other side. "You remember me, Mr. O'Brian?"

"Why would I?"

"Memphis. At Aunt Martha's."

"Okay."

Buddy patted Mojo on the head to signal it was not a stranger and opened the door. "Come on in."

"Don't want to catch you at a bad time." The door clicked as Detective Allen closed it behind him.

"It's cool." Buddy walked back into the living room and placed his guitar on the coffee table. Judging from his shadow, Buddy figured the detective to be abut his height, around 5'10, and probably in his mid to late 30s. Picking a shirt off the back of the sofa, Buddy slipped it on. "Sit down."

"Your RV was ransacked a couple of days ago."

"I reported it to the Baton Rouge police." Buddy sat on the edge of the sofa and ran his hand across the scar and the stubble on his cheek. "They call a Memphis cop for that?"

"No, Mr. O'Brian, not for that. Least not on its own." Detective Allen's voice was polite, quiet.

"What then?"

"I think the people that did it were looking for something that might have a connection to the murder of Jake Washington."

Buddy leaned toward the voice. "I don't know what you're after, but I'm clean. I haven't done drugs for five years now, I don't own a gun or an ice pick and I barely knew Jake Washington. I use the RV to stay in when I'm on the road because I don't do well alone in strange motel rooms."

"How about your singer, Nina Boxer? Anything between the two of you? She was using."

"Nina's not my girl and she's not with my group anymore." Buddy heard the agitation in his tone and so did Mojo, who growled deep in his throat. Buddy reached down to pat the dog's head. "I let her go."

"When was that?"

"Couple days ago. What'd you want from me, detective?"

Buddy could feel the policeman move forward in the white chair with the poppy red pillow. Allen's voice was tense when he asked, "That the last time you spoke to her?"

"Yeah. Except I phoned her yesterday morning." Buddy buttoned the bottom of his shirt, suddenly feeling undressed.

"Nina Boxer is dead. She was murdered last night around midnight."

Buddy's fingers froze on the button. He drew his breath in so sharply that Mojo got to his feet and pushed up against Buddy's leg.

"Someone killed Nina?"

"Stuck an ice pick in her ear. Just like Jake Washington."

"An ice pick---holy shit!" Buddy reached out to touch Mojo, digging his fingers into the dog's hair, holding on. He realized the detective was still speaking.

"More than just a coincidence, don't you think?" Allen got to his feet and Buddy stood up. "I got a warrant and we're going over your Winnebago now for fingerprints or anything else that might help."

"They walked across the room where Allen stopped, opened the door, and turned to Buddy. "If I were you, I'd be careful."

After the door closed, Buddy stood there without moving, his bare feet sinking into the carpet, his hands flat against the legs of his jeans. He remembered Nina in the days when the two of them were using; rising up and floating on cocaine high late at night after the gig was over. He felt her thin body and full lips close to him in the motel beds in cities with forgotten names. Then Ivy left him and wouldn't come back until he went to rehab. He didn't think he could live without Ivy. She was all that kept him from drifting away and drowning in the murky waters of a world where illusion was easier than reality. It was a time when music and drugs and the moment were the place he lived and life didn't begin until after midnight and the first sniff of white powder or a sweet shooter of Jack Daniels warmed his blood. He knew if he lost Ivy, he would lose his way.

Nina begged him to stay with her. In sober moments back then, he realized the danger of going on along that road. So he endured agonizing weeks of detox and Nina disappeared. Letting go of the cocaine was hard, but not nearly as hard as the call of dark whiskey and its tease of mellow relief. Nina didn't return until six months ago when she showed up, swearing she was clean and sober and wanted her old job back.

"Jesus," he whispered. "An ice pick."

**

Nina's funeral was held at the Church of the Nazarene on North Street where her family had attended services for twenty years. The black congregation turned out to support Lisa Boxer and secretly shook their heads over the wild life her daughter, Nina, had led and how she died.

"Lisa did her best, bless her heart," members whispered.

"Get mixed up with those musicians and that's what happens," they said.

"It's a wild life with all that drugs and music mess."

"Girl that pretty is always wild from the start. Men after her all the time."

"Well, she's in the arms of The Lamb now."

Pastor Williams preached a full sermon on how Christ died for our sins and now Nina was safe in His Kingdom, away from the wicked temptations of the world. Safe in the arms of Jesus, Nina would not endure any more hardship or pain.

Ladies of the congregation brought casseroles, baked hams, fried chicken, chocolate and coconut cakes, berry pies, pecan pies and peach cobblers. In the basement of the little building, Buddy and his band sat up drums and a keyboard to play for the reception.

Men took off their suit coats and loosened their ties, young girls kicked off their high-heel shoes, and children chased each other across the room, their shouts echoing across the hall. Musicians from all over town joined in to pay tribute to one of their own. A church deacon passed the collection plate to help Nina's family with the expense of her burial. Buddy took a hundred dollar bill from his wallet and whispered to Ivy to throw it in when the plate came by.

Ivy crooned *I'll Be Seeing You* with Franklin accompanying her on the keyboard. Members of the church choir sang *His Eye Is On The Sparrow* and *Swing Low, Sweet Chariot*.

Nina went out with more style than she had lived, Buddy thought. Still, the people who knew her got up before the audience and recalled only the good things about her.

"Prettiest girl on the block."

"Voice like an angel."

"Got her start right here in our church choir."

Buddy played *Trying to Cry You Back Home*, singing it in his raspy voice and struggling not to falter when his throat tightened. After a couple of hours, people began to drift away, picking up their empty dishes, scraping leftover desserts onto paper plates to leave for those who stayed, and hauling sleepy children out to waiting cars. When they were the only ones left, the musicians played on, jamming together, forgetting why they were there, just lost in their music and the bond of those who shared it. Buddy thought how Nina would have loved to be there, cupping her hand around the microphone, her slender body swaying in a tight silver dress, singing an old blues song.

When the musicians began breaking up, putting their instruments in cases, shaking hands and saying goodbye, Buddy put his Gibson away and turned toward Eldon's voice.

"Franklin, take me over where Eldon is," he said.

"Sure Buddy." Franklin took his elbow and they walked across the room, Mojo close to Buddy's side.

"Well hey, Buddy," Eldon said as they approached him. "This' a sad, sad day."

"It is."

Franklin gave Buddy's elbow a squeeze. "I'm going over to get some ice tea. Just call if you need me."

He left the two standing near the wall, where metal folding chairs were being stacked beside them with a loud clatter.

"Well, I remember when that little girl first came to us. She was green as could be. You remember how she was? Trying to sing some Motown songs that didn't suit her at all? No, not at all." Eldon would have rattled on but Buddy stopped him.

"You get that studio reserved yet?"

"Well now, Buddy, this business can wait until another time--."

"I might as well tell you, Eldon. I'm breaking our contract as of now."

"What are you talking about? What for? "

"I'm reasonably sure, Eldon, that you've been skimming off the top."

"Now you hold on," Eldon's voice took a hard edge, losing the usual good old boy drawl. "This is not the place for that kind of talk."

"Good as any. A place for sayin' goodbye."

"You got no call to say I'm a cheat."

"You've been taking off the top for a while now. Suspected that you were, but yesterday I talked to Jake Washington's people. That check you gave me just don't add up straight. I'm blind, Eldon, not stupid."

Mojo became alert, pushing his body between the two men.

"I'd kick your ass for talkin' to me like that, but you'd sic that crazy dog on me."

"Take your shot."

Mojo snarled, bearing his teeth.

"I'll just sue you instead."

"Not unless you want to answer to a felony charge that I'll bring against you for embezzlement."

"Go to Hell, you blind bastard. You wouldn't be anywhere if it hadn't been for me. You're a used up has-been anyway." Eldon stalked away, Mojo's snarl following him.

"Has been maybe," Buddy said, more to himself than Eldon's back. "But not used up yet."

"What was that about?" Ivy said, touching Buddy on the arm.

"Hey baby." He turned to her and smiled. "Did I tell you how pretty you look tonight?"

"How would you know?" she said, laughing and leaning into him.

"I like the way you did that song too." Buddy wrapped his arms around her. "I think you got a future in the music business."

"Buddy," she said against his jacket, "did that detective say Nina was killed by the same person that murdered Jake Washington?"

"Said there may be a connection."

"Does he think you had something to do with it?"

"No. He thinks I'm next."

Chapter Seven

When they were home again, Buddy took off his coat and tie then threw them across the back of the sofa. He slipped out of his loafers and stood still for a moment. The funeral was over, but he could almost feel Nina; see her laughing; hear her crooning a sad blues song into the mike. He turned and walked to the small upright piano near the wall and sat down on the bench. The keys felt cool to his touch as he ran his fingers across them. He was conscious of Ivy giving Mojo his dinner, talking to him in a soothing voice, telling him what a good dog he was. Buddy began to play *But Not for Me*, the kind of show tune that jazz musicians love to do, taking the melody and then wandering off on his own into a world of innovation. He heard Ivy settle onto a nearby chair to listen, but he played for himself, searching the cords that suited his mood.

"You should have stayed with the piano," Ivy said.

When they released Buddy from the hospital after he lost most of sight in the street fight, Jimmy had driven Buddy to the Missouri School for the Blind where the court had ordered him to stay for the next two years.

"Sure and it's a grand place, my lad," Jimmy had tried to reassure his son. "The building is big as an Irish castle."

Buddy said nothing; he just followed his father down halls filled with voices and footsteps.

"'Tis' ours here," said Jimmy, stopping. "Room 209."

They put the few things that Buddy brought with him in the two drawers allotted to him from a four-drawer chest and hung his clothes in the half of the small closet he would share with a roommate. Then they sat together on the small bunk that was to be his until he left the school at age eighteen. Neither of them spoke. They had cried all their tears. Jimmy had lost his beautiful Yvette and now his son would be hundreds of miles away.

Buddy, in his world of lines and shadows, would live in a place as foreign to him as Africa. So they just waited until the bell sounded and the voice over the loud speaker told them all visitors must leave.

They stood up to say good-bye and Jimmy placed a thin chain over Buddy's head so that a small pendent hung against his chest.

"'Tis Saint Patrick, the patron saint of Ireland," Jimmy said. "He will keep you safe while you are here."

Buddy, determined not to cry, felt tears crowding his eyes as his father held him in a hard embrace and muttered, "The saints be with you boy."

Then he was gone and Buddy felt completely alone. He could hear the doors slamming, voices laughing and shouting, and footsteps echoing along the halls. He just sat there on the bunk and waited in the semi-darkness. A shadow moved toward him through the open door and a voice said, "Hi, I'm Kevin, your roommate. They told me you were here. Take my arm and we'll go down to dinner."

"People call me Buddy." He reached for an arm, moving his hand until he connected with it. "Are you blind?"

"Yeah, but this is my second year here. I can find my way around pretty well. It doesn't take long."

Maybe it would be better, Buddy thought as he followed Kevin through the halls, to be completely blind than in this shadow world of his.

"You like it here?"

"It's not bad," Kevin said. "Lots of things to do. I play trombone in the school band. You play an instrument?"

"I play the piano some," Buddy said.

"I'll introduce you to the band teacher."

The people at the school were kind, strict, and without pity. When he asked to play in the band, they said there was already a good piano player, but there was a place for someone who could play the guitar. Could he do that?

Buddy took the instrument they put in his hands and ran his fingers over the frets, instantly in love. "Yes, I can."

Through the years of long days spent learning and nights spent dreaming, the guitar was always within Buddy's reach. During classes of Braille, English, and math, the hard instrument case leaned against his desk. In quiet hours, he sat on his bunk and practiced. Jimmy brought him music tapes and Buddy listened to them over and over, imitating the great blues guitarists. In music class and at band practice he was happy, lost in a world of cords and rhythm. In the time space after school and before dinner, the sightless musicians would jam together in the band room. Kevin became his best friend, along with Rhonda, a girl who played the clarinet and loved to laugh. Just the way Yvette, Buddy remembered, had loved to laugh. One day, in their senior year, he had backed Rhonda against the music room wall and kissed her. She did not laugh then.

"You are a blind musician Buddy. Music is where your heart is," she said. "One kiss is all I can give you."

The school's band went on the road, playing in competitions across the United States. With complete certainty Buddy knew this was what he wanted to do forever. And now, fifteen years later, he was still doing it.

"Remember this one?" he asked Ivy now, as he played an old Johnny Mercer song.

"It's beautiful," she said.

"Ivy, call tomorrow and set up a recording studio so we can began putting together the new CD."

"Okay."

"Come over here now and I'll teach you the new songs you'll be doing."

Ivy moved over to the bench beside him. "Buddy, did that detective really say you could be next?"

"Yep."

"Why? What have you done?"

"Beats the hell out of me. My guitar playing couldn't be that bad. Might be my singing." He began playing a melody, memory leading his fingers across the piano keys. "Here now, listen to this and then we'll sing the words together."

It was how he liked them to be, Ivy singing the lead while he backed her up, blending his raspy voice with her smoky one. He had hopes for this song. The lyrics had come from someplace inside him, part of a secret dream he never acknowledged.

"That's a great song," Ivy said. "What'd you name it?"

"*Last Call.*" He closed the lid down on the piano. He took Ivy by the hand and they walked down the hall to the bedroom. Ivy went into the bathroom to brush her teeth, leaving the door open and telling him she was excited about the new songs, saying she thought he was in a different musical faze. Buddy sat on the side of the bed, waiting for her, hearing the tap water running, imagining her washing her face and slipping a satin night gown over her head.

"Ivy, I need you to manage the band."

"I can't do that."

"I fired Eldon today."

"What? Why?"

"He was skimming, Ivy. I need someone I can trust. I need you to go on the road with me."

She was walking toward him now, her shadow over him. "I have a job. I can't go on the road."

"Quit your job. We can make enough money. I know I can pay you more than you're making now."

"No. No Buddy, I can't do that."

"If you love me enough, you'll do this for me."

He reached for her hand but she pulled back.

"If I love you enough? Ever since we were sixteen years old I've given my life to you and now you want my security too. How much more? You'll consume me if I let you."

"That's pretty dramatic isn't it? All I'm asking is that you come into business with me."

"And stand in your shadow and be your eyes and ears and general flunky."

"How can you look at it like that? I'm offering you a business deal." He didn't understand where all the anger was coming from.

"You want me to give up my job, my club dates, and yes, my friends. In other words, any life I have without you."

"Come on baby, that's not..."

"Yes it is. You want me to sing blues, not jazz. It's as if anything I want doesn't matter. I'm not a person, Buddy, I'm just an extension of you. " Her voice choked over the words.

Buddy felt slapped. He stood up, trying to reconcile this angry woman with the soft-spoken Ivy who had laughed him through troubled times, held his hand and whispered to him in the lowest moments; been the oak tree he clung to.

"Take the bed," she grabbed a pillow and it brushed his arm as she pulled it to her. "I'll sleep in the other room."

Chapter Eight

"Stop! Stop!" Buddy quit playing in the middle of a riff and raised his arm.

He could sense Rufus, Strum, Amos and Franklin looking at him, their hands paused on their instruments. He could feel their frustration at doing the song over and over, but he wanted it to be right, to tell the story the way it had to be told.

"What's wrong now?" Strum asked. He'd be sitting on a chair, the bass guitar resting on a crossed leg. "Man, you're killing us. This is the fifth time you stopped. This rate, we goanna be here all night."

Rufus quieted the symbol with one hand, his drum sticks in the other. Franklin banged the flat of his hand against the piano.

"What'd you want from us, Buddy?" Franklin asked. "What're we doin' wrong?"

"Don't try to jump this song," Buddy said. "It has some class; some sophistication. Think of Sinatra with his hat tipped back; it's bar closing time and he's missing his woman. Put some pain in it."

"Thought we was doing that already," Strum mumbled.

"Sinatra ain't no blues singer," Rufus said. "Got no soul."

"I don't want your soul, just the hole in it. Rufus, give me some brushes," Buddy said. "Let's go again."

The piano came in softly, brushes moved against the drums, and guitars carried the rhythm. Buddy sang:

It's our last call
It's our last call, darlin'
It's the last call for you and me

This time, he noted, there was a little more of what he wanted in the piano, a lighter touch to the drum, and depth in the bass. He sang from

31

some dark place inside him, making the guitar cry, keeping the cords mellow. Ivy would come to the studio alone and record the harmony later, let the mixer blend the voices. Their argument last week in their bedroom had hung there between them, leaving a hollow feeling inside him and a cold space between them as they went through each day like strangers. She kept her distance and he struggled to understand her outrage. He sang from that place where her anger left him waiting.

When the clock strikes two
It's the end of me and you
It's our last call

Buddy put his hand up and brought it down. The song ended with brushes against symbols.

"That's it," he said, pushing his guitar pick between the strings and placing the instrument on the floor. "Let's wrap it. I think we got it right that time."

Buddy could hear them grumbling, see their shadows as they put their instruments away. "That's it for today, Carl," he said to the man in the sound booth. "We can work on the mix tomorrow."

Franklin closed the piano down with a light thud. "We all finished with this? Cause I need to help my dad out with a house tomorrow."

"Boy, you a musician or a carpenter?" Strum said.

"Carpenter work pays the bills," returned Franklin. "I don't got a wife like you, working in a hospital and bringing home the rent."

"Watch your mouth now, boy."

Rufus was taking the symbols apart and they rang as he dropped them in their case. "Don't know about you cats but I need to get back to some club work, my bank account is tapped out. Maybe letting Eldon go was not a good idea."

"You got anything booked, man?" Strum was standing a few feet from Buddy.

"Ivy's working on it now. Got some things in the discussion stage," Buddy said. "We finish this CD, we'll work plenty."

"I'm splitting, catch you later," Franklin said. "You comin' Amos?"

"Right behind you."

Buddy walked closer to the shadow he knew was Strum. "You got a couple of joints?"

"You crazy? I'm not giving you anything to get you back using again. You got a way home? 'Cause I'm leaving now."

"Go on." Hell with him, Buddy thought. Self-righteous bastard did a joint every night. No one accused him of being a junkie.

"I'll carry you on home Buddy," Rufus said. "Wait 'till I pack up."

Buddy put his guitar in its case and zipped it closed. "Can you drop me by Jimmy's?"

"No sweat."

Buddy reached out and put his hand on the drummer's arm. "You got any weed?"

"You sure, man? You ain't getting' started again are you?"

"Just to keep in my pocket."

Rufus' laugh was quiet and low. "Don't have anything on me, but if you really are in need, go to the Good Night motel on the edge of Spanish Town and tell the night clerk I said you should come there."

Chapter Nine

There was about half a dozen men at the bar. Buddy could hear the low rumble of their voices, punctuated with sharp laughter. The rattle of dice against a cup and the slap of a palm against the bar-top added to the rhythm of an old do-wop tune playing over the jukebox.

Mojo led Buddy to an empty stool and as he settled on it, someone slapped his shoulder.

"Good to see you boy. Remember me, Earl Thomas?"

"Hey Buddy, how ya doin'? Tom Jordan here."

"What's up kid? Bill Locke over here."

Buddy had known them since childhood. They'd drunk at Jimmy's bar as long as he could remember; Jimmy setting up more free drinks than they paid for. They ate the pretzels and nuts out of little plastic bowls while they downed beer and repeated over and over the same old war stories about life in the neighborhood when they were young. They talked of their service in Vietnam and grumbled about how America did them wrong when they came home. He could almost see them in their work clothes as they pushed buttons on the jukebox that played songs from the sixties. He could smell the dirt, paint dust, and sweat that still clung to them after eight hours on the job. Blue collar Southerners, the men took pride in Buddy as if they were his uncles and he could feel their strong sense of family reach out and include him. He was theirs as much as their own brother's kid might be. A hand took Buddy's and wrapped it around a glass.

"Seven-up and lemon for my lad. 'Tis fine to see you this day."

"Thanks Jimmy. We've been recording for the last three days. I'm really tired."

He sipped from the glass, tasting the sweet, icy drink, wishing it had the smooth bite of whiskey. He felt like crying as old emotions came rising to the surface in this place he would always call home, where these men made him welcome.

Someone pushed a cup to him, bumping his hand. "How 'bout I roll you for the next drink?"

"Don't think you can cheat me now," Buddy laughed, "Mojo'll read the dice for me."

After a couple of games of liar's dice, Buddy bought the bar a drink, picking a bill from his wallet where they were placed in order of value, the twenties folded at the left corner. Mojo lay beside the stool, accepting a few pats on the head but refusing to take the pretzels offered to him by anyone except his owner.

"Play some old ragtime piano like you did when you was a kid," Bill Locke said.

"Naw, not today. My voice is tired from recording."

"I'll sing you a ballad," Jimmy said.

"We can hear you anytime." Locke and the others laughed.

"It would still be better than a washed-up blues singer." A voice from the end of the bar spoke.

Mojo growled low in his throat. The laughter stopped and there was a strained silence.

"I think you found the wrong bar, mister," Jimmy spoke up. "Finish up and leave."

"Let it go Eldon" Buddy said, recognizing his ex-manager's voice.

"Hear you're recording," Eldon was suddenly at Buddy's shoulder. "We still got a contract."

"Take me to court." Buddy turned on his stool to face the shadow.

"I'll take you to your grave, you blind punk."

Mojo was on his feet, brushing close to Buddy as he got off the bar stool. Buddy's hand closed around the switch blade knife he carried in his pocket. It was an old habit from his days on the streets and it felt as familiar now as it had then.

"You want to back away Eldon."

"I hear you're trying to book some club work. I'll make sure you never get another gig around here."

"I'm having you audited Eldon. See what you control from the county slam." His thumb found the button on the knife.

"You double-crossing low life," Eldon grabbed Buddy's shirt.

Bar-stools scraped on the floor as men jumped to their feet, but before they could get to Eldon, Mojo made a leap, knocking the man to the floor with eighty pounds of muscle and snarl. Jimmy was yelling for Buddy to call Mojo off and Eldon was screaming.

"Mojo! Heel."

Mojo retreated to stand beside his master, the growl low in his throat. Buddy could hear Bill Locke and Earl Thomas cursing Eldon as they pulled him to his feet and walked him to the door. He heard a scuffle and Eldon saying "Let go. Get your hands off me."

It was quiet for a moment and then, "I'll take care of you later, Buddy."

"On my terms, Eldon."

"What's that?'

"You and me in a phone booth with straight razors."

"Crazy son-of-a-bitch."

"Down Mojo," Buddy calmed the dog.

The door slammed behind Eldon and there wasn't a sound in the room. Bar fights were not common at Jimmy O'Brian's, at least not anymore. But some had been deadly back in the days when Yvette danced and laughed across the barroom, men had come to blows over her, fighting for just a dance or a smile. Jimmy had tangled with more than one man who refused to walk away.

"Drinks on the house my lads," called Jimmy.

The men went back to their places, Jimmy pouring fresh beer from the tap. The mugs made a whizzing sound as they slid down the bar. The drinkers were quiet now; Buddy knew some were glancing sideways at the dog, others keeping their eyes on their beer.

Buddy took the leash and patted Mojo. "Good boy."

"What's the pleasure here?" called Jimmy as he put coins in the jukebox and pushed some buttons. The Grateful Dead began to play a tune about working men, and someone rattled the dice cup.

"Bill, could you see if there's a taxi at the corner?" Buddy asked. "I need to get going."

"Sure thing. Just tell the dog, its okay." Bill Locke took Buddy's arm, walking him out onto the sidewalk. "Old Bradley's down on the corner, sitting in his cab reading the newspaper as usual. Let's get you in there and I'll tell him not to be cheatin' you on the fare."

In the back seat of Bradley's cab, Buddy leaned forward and said, "The Good Night Motel, you know where that is?"

The driver laughed and pulled the car away from the curb. "Popular place if you're looking for anything but a good night's sleep."

"Stop at the first place you see. I want a fifth."

It was a short ride inside the cab that smelled like body sweat, stale coffee and onions. The cab pulled over and Bradley asked "You want me to go in for you?"

"Yeah." Buddy picked a bill from his wallet and handed it over the seat. "Jack Daniels. Black label. This right?"

"Yeah." The twenty with the backward fold moved from his hand. "Be right back."

Bradley returned with a paper bag and handed it over the seat. "Good Night Motel?"

"That's right."

Half a block later, the cab pulled to a stop. "Want me to take you in?"

"We'll be okay." Buddy and Mojo stepped onto the drive- through and he could make out the image of an entry. Mojo led him into the office where the pungent smell of curry clung to the wall.

"Need a single?" a voice asked. "How long?"

"Yeah, gimme a room. I don't know how long." Buddy figured the voice belonged to an East Indian man, maybe in his early twenties.

"One night in advance."

"Need something else. Rufus said you could help out."

"How you know Rufus?"

"He's my drummer. I'm Buddy O'Brian with Mojo's Blues Band."

"Oh yeah, I know who you are. I love the blues. They call you Blind Buddy. That's cool. What's your poison?"

"Coupla joints. And later I might want to send out for a bottle." Buddy took several bills from his wallet and placed them on the counter. "Until this is gone."

A low whistle, then, "be right back."

Buddy waited, patting Mojo on the head, anticipation growing inside him. He remembered the dream world where a man could go any time he wanted, forget anything, be anything. He was anxious to be there again where he could forget the quarrel with Ivy, the fight with Eldon, and not worry about getting the band back to work.

When the clerk returned, he took Buddy by the arm as if to lead him, but jerked back when Mojo growled.

"We'll follow you," Buddy said. "What's your name?"

"Sanjay Sing. I work nights, you need anything else, wait for me to come on shift."

They walked down the outside of the cinder block building with the crunch of gravel under their feet until the clerk stopped and unlocked a door, pushing it open. Mojo and Buddy stepped inside to a musky smell, and he could imagine a faded bed spread covering a sagging mattress against a bedpost nailed to the wall.

"Bathroom to your left. I'm laying your key and package here on the table."

"Bring me glass from the bathroom and a bucket of ice from your machine."

"Sure."

"Put the package in my hand. Lighter too."

"Yeah, sure thing." He took Buddy's hand and placed an envelope in it. "Need anything, call the house phone. Just pick it up and push the last button. Can you do that?"

"Order me a pizza, will you? Any kind. And a fifth of Jack Daniels black label. There enough money left for that?"

"Yeah. You a friend of Rufus, a big blues star and all. I'll bring it down myself."

"Make sure the door locks on your way out."

When the door closed behind the clerk, Buddy kicked off his loafers and then sat down at the round table in the corner of the room. He took the bottle from the paper bag and opened it slowly, careful not to spill a drop of the dark magic inside.

Chapter Ten

The rattling door knob sounded like a blast of thunder. Mojo was barking and the pain in his head ripped his brain like a hot knife. Quiet, he wanted call out, quiet. He knew they were there, but he was somewhere else and he wanted to stay there. Go away, he thought, go away.

"How the hell long has he been here?"

Face down on the bed, Buddy he could make out Strum's deep voice through the fog in his head. .

The desk clerk answered with an annoying whine. "Five days. Thought I'd better call Rufus 'cause I didn't want him to die in the motel. You that big-shot bass player, ain't you?"

"Damm, he stinks," Strum said. "Help me get him into the shower."

"That dog'll jump us if we touch him."

Mojo was whining and barking. Strum was soothing him, saying "Good boy, Mojo. We gonna take care of Buddy now, don't worry."

"Seems to like you."

"Knows me. Jes get his other arm and help me drag him in the bathroom. Close the door so the dog can't get in."

Buddy felt himself being lifted from the bed, his body was dead weight and he was unable command it to move. He heard Mojo bark and tried to call to him but his tongue wouldn't work. His mind was still in that dark place, not wanting to return, fighting the light. Somewhere it seemed as if a demon laughed and the air was thick and muggy around him. His bare feet moved across the floor but he was not walking. They were dragging him between them and the carpet scraped against his toes. Hands were pulling at his jeans and shirt, taking them off. He tried to push away, but his brain wouldn't work, couldn't control his limbs from the dark place he was in. When the cold water hit his head, the shock brought him back. He yelled out and tried to fight back, flailing his arms at them and catching only air. Under the cascade of icy water and the thumping, thumping, as Mojo threw his weight against the door, barking and clawing, wanting to get to him, he thought he would go crazy. The iron hands held Buddy in that icy waterfall until the demon retreated and his mind began to clear to a hazy mist.

Mercifully, they turned off the water and threw a towel at his head. He felt weak and his hands shook as he tried to dry his face, water dripping from his thick hair. Inside his head the world was twisting and turning, doing the hangover dance. He swayed on his feet; he needed a drink. Where was that damn bottle?

"You'll have to put those clothes back on," Strum said. "Get you home, you can clean yourself up."

Buddy held on to the wall, sliding down the rough surface to the cool tile floor. Strum's voice was clearer now. The bathroom door opened and Mojo ran in, prodding him with his nose and brushing up against him, licking his face.

"Must have drunk five bottles of Jack," Strum was saying. "Empties everywhere. Pizza boxes on the floor, that what you been feeding Mojo all this time? Bet you glad to see me, ain't ya boy?"

"He'd let the dog out a couple times a day, I seen him do that," the clerk said, the whine still in his voice. "People started complaining about a big dog like that out in the parking lot, doing his business and all. I finally called Rufus. Why didn't he come?"

"He called me." Strum said. "Help me get him to the car."

"Owes me some for the room."

"He musta given you money in advance." Strum, holding Buddy around the waist now to keep him upright, pulled a twenty dollar bill from his pocket and threw it on the floor. "You not running a scam on me now, are you son?"

"Well—being you're Rusfus' friend, big blues star and all, I'll let it ride." He reached down and picked up the money.

"Good man. Now open the door." Strum was dragging Buddy across the floor. Mojo barked a couple of times and Buddy could feel the dog moving beside him. The sudden blast of sunlight hurt and he put his hands up to shield his head from the brightness and heat. Strum shoved him into the passenger seat of his old Toyota and Mojo jumped into the back.

"Want to go home or to your daddy's place?"

"Jimmy's."

Facing Ivy right now, in this condition, would be more than he could handle. She might leave him for sure this time, might not come back like she did before. Couldn't beg her to stay, it wasn't in him to do that and if she went away, he knew he would slip off into that world, that deep pit of despair. This time he might not return.

The movement of the car made his head pound and his stomach boiled with nausea. Rolling down the window, feeling the warm air on his face, he tried to hang on. The world spun in bright colors while amplified street noises reverberated in his head. Stop! He wanted to call out. Stop!

"Don't throw up in my car now," Strum cautioned. "We'll be there in a minute."

Jimmy came out to help haul him into the apartment behind the bar. "Good God boy, what have ya been up to?"

"Give me a drink Jimmy."

"You had way too much."

"Just to clear my head." A tremor ran through his body and every part of him began to shake as if he were freezing.

"He' gonna have to sleep it off," Strum was pushing him toward a bed. "Better lock him in here."

"Looks like he might be going into the DTs. He's shaking like a leaf." There was concern in Jimmy's voice and his Irish brogue thickened.

"Jest give me a drink."

"All right, one shooter to put you to sleep." Jimmy held a shot glass to Buddy's lips and the magic liquid slid down his throat, claming the seizure.

"Help me pull off these clothes, they smell like rotten cabbage." Jimmy was jerking at Buddy's pants. They left him naked on the bed and he felt Mojo jump up beside him. He heard the lock click on the door before the darkness dragged him back again.

When he woke he could smell gardenias and he knew Ivy was there, sitting in the easy chair nearby. His naked body was covered by a cotton sheet and big band music was playing in the other room. Mojo's weight pressed against his leg at the foot of the bed.

"Am I home?" he asked.

"You're in your old bedroom at Jimmy's."

He knew it now; the smell of boiled cabbage and potatoes and rich coffee. The Benny Goodman music Jimmy played when no one else was listening. The room he grew up in probably still had the Eric Clapton poster on the wall, his cheap stereo on top of the dresser, and mud stained cleats in the corner.

"You need to eat. Jimmy made potato soup."

"Ivy." He raised his hand but it was trembling, so he put it down. The thought of rich, chunky potato soup made him ill. "Just a glass of cold milk and some aspirin."

"Okay, I'll get it."

He sat up in bed, threw his legs over the side and stood up. The shaking stayed with him and he felt weak as he lurched forward, sliding against the wall, barely making it into the bathroom. He relieved himself and turned on the cold water, splashing his face over and over. Fumbling in the drawer beneath the sink, he found an old toothbrush and cleaned his mouth, washing away the bad taste that filled it. God! What he'd give for a drink.

Ivy came in as he staggered back into the bedroom. She put three aspirin in his hand and when he popped them in his mouth, she gave him the glass of milk. The liquid was cool and comforting and he drank it in two long swallows. He sat on the bed and pulled the sheet across his lap. Ivy sat down beside him.

"They finished mixing the CD a couple of days ago and they're getting it ready for distribution."

"Ivy, I—"

"Buddy, it's good. It's really good. *Last Call's* the best thing you've ever done."

He didn't know what to say, so he just sat there, wanting to laugh, wanting to say he knew it would be. But his head ached and his stomach was queasy and he was shaking.

"Can I have a drink? You know, a hair of the dog?"

"Do you understand what I'm saying? This could put you on top again."

He didn't know how to answer her, wasn't sure what she said. As soon as the aspirin stopped the pounding in his head he would understand her.

"Damn you, Buddy." There was anger in her voice now. "Why do you try to kill yourself like this? Why do you have to ruin everything?"

He just sat on the bed, holding his pounding head, stripped of his clothes, stripped of his dignity, saying nothing.

"I would have left for good this time no matter how much I love you. But I have an investment in this CD too. My time and my voice are there."

"Don't go," he whispered.

Ivy waited a moment and then said. "I took a six month leave from my job so I can manage you, that's how much I believe in this CD."

He wanted to hold her, to kiss her hair and neck and say he loved her, but he was too sick, too weak. When she brushed his cheeks with her fingertips, he realized she was wiping away his tears.

Taking her hand, he held her fingers to his lips and murmured, "I love you Ivy. Let's go home."

"You've got to pull yourself together. As soon as you feel stronger, we'll go home." She ran her free hand across his curls. "We've got a lot of work ahead of us."

"The guys are grumbling about money." The pounding in his head eased some, leaving a dull ache.

"I have us booked into the Denim and Blues this Saturday night. We'll do some of the new songs."

"That's three steps above the places we've been working."

"Double the money too."

"How'd you do that?"

"My beauty and charm. Think you can make it?"

"If I have to crawl or ride on Mojo's back."

"Long as you can sit on a chair and hold a guitar. But I want you to know that if you pull another bender and mess up this up, I'm gone for good."

Chapter Eleven

Ivy's smoky voice filled the room. She leaned into the microphone and sang in that throaty, intimate way of hers, causing the audience to hush, not wanting to miss a word. Buddy had written the song, he knew every phrase, every note. Still, when she sang it with such feeling, he found he was listening like the rest of the audience to the intensity of her voice and the bending of his lyrics.

The Diamonds and Blues club was packed and he could hear waiters moving around the tables, whispering drink orders, and ice rattling against glasses as they placed them on tables. No one danced, but stayed seated at round tables covered with white cloths and flickering candles in small hurricane lamps. Cigarette smoke floated up onto the stage where the band sat and people murmured when they talked. In places like this, Buddy knew, people wore expensive denim and ordered scotch and soda or vodka martinis. They paid the bill with a Visa card and someone else parked their car and brought it back to the door when they were ready to leave. Buddy was reasonably sure there would be no fights in this club's parking lot tonight. Hell, they even had a dressing room for the musicians, as if blues band members changed clothes for a performance. Only Ivy used it, the rest of them spent their time between sets standing out behind the building, Strum and Rufus sharing a joint, Buddy and Franklin drinking Dr. Peppers. Amos always joined a woman waiting for him at the bar.

"I hate playing these stuck up places," Rufus took a toke and passed the joint on to Strum. "These people are pretenders. Don't know crap about what they're listening to."

"Pay's better," Buddy said. "And we got two more weekends here."

"Ain't a real blues club."

Buddy heard the pop as Rufus opened a can of beer.

"We need someone to get knifed in the parking lot to make it real?" Franklin said.

"Shut up kid. Whatta you know?" Rufus threw his can into a trash bin and it banged against the rim. "We had a good circuit we was working. Always felt welcome."

"You like the money, don't you Rufus?" Franklin threw his Dr. Pepper can toward the bin. It hit the lip and crashed to the pavement with tinny sound.

"Should have kept Eldon managing us. Kept things like they were." Rufus grumbled.

Buddy didn't want to get into it with the disgruntled drummer, so he let that remark go by. He knew Rufus had never liked Ivy and sure as hell didn't take to having her be band boss. We'll, he'd just have to live with it or leave.

"Let's get back to the stand." Buddy put his hand on Franklin's shoulder and followed him through the door, Mojo walking along beside.

It was popular now to love the blues, like society had once loved jazz, because there was a rebellious wild feel to it. Buddy remembered a time when the same people had looked down on the blues, considering it black ghetto music. Now he smiled as Ivy finished her song in the last set and the audience stood applauding and yelling things like bravo and encore! He knew she added class to the band with her cross-over style.

"Ivy Martin, ladies and gentlemen," Buddy said as her shadow walked off stage. "If you like that song, it's on our new CD. You can pick up a copy at that table by the door. "

The band went right into that blues standard *Kansas City* and loud applause erupted from the crowd. Buddy leaned forward and sang in his raspy voice while Franklin played a rowdy roadhouse style on the piano. Buddy could feel the floor vibrate as people danced to this popular old favorite. After that, he let Strum take over with some front porch blues while he sat back and thought about the conversation in the ally.

Buddy didn't know what was eating Rufus. He'd been moody ever since he had fired Eldon and Ivy had taken over as manager. He kept complaining about staying too close to Baton Rouge, saying he liked going on the road, playing the old clubs. Didn't like the class of people in the uptown places they were booked into now, saying they were out of their element. His attitude had began to grind on Buddy who felt that now they were moving back into the mainstream, even crossing over with that new song "Last Call." Still, Rufus was a good blues drummer and most of the band's songs were carried by his steady, straight ahead beat. He'd been with Buddy for two years now and never missed a gig.

At then end of *Kansas City*" the band went right into *Trying to Cry You Back Home* and Buddy reminded the audience that they were Mojo's Blues Band. "Thank ya'll for coming out tonight and we'll be back next Saturday evening for more blues and good times."

At places like Aunt Martha's he would have said blues and booze and a bell would have rang announcing the last call for alcohol. But not here where a musician's tip jar was not allowed and people ordered call drinks and designated a skimpy gratuity for the waiters when they signed their names on the bill, leaving no cash on the table.

At the end of the set, Diamonds and Blues patrons came up to the stage to meet the musicians. As usual, several young girls were making a beeline for Franklin and Amos who disappeared with some classy woman. Aspiring guitarists crowded a grumpy Strum to ask questions. Others pushed CDs or photos at them to sign.

"Enjoyed your music tonight, Buddy." The shadow stood in front of Buddy. "Followed your career for a couple of years and wondered what happened to you."

Buddy put out his hand in the general direction. "Didn't go no place. I've been here, mostly on tour. Got a new CD and we played some of it tonight."

A firm hand grasped his and a bass voice said, "Name's Art Kimble. I own a radio station called KBLZ. New in Baton Rouge and I'm planning on making it a blues station as you can tell by the name."

"Sounds good."

"We can set up an on-air interview if you're interested."

"You need to talk to Ivy. She's the manager."

"You mean that hot looking singer?"

The remark irritated Buddy so he reached behind him and picked his guitar off the chair. He slid the pick he was holding between the frets and started to slide the instrument into the soft case. "She takes care of all the business."

"Well maybe the two of you will join me for a late supper or early breakfast. There's a place about a block down where we can talk."

"Call us tomorrow." Buddy put the instrument case on his shoulder. "Strum, give this guy a card will you?"

"Here, I've got one." Ivy was there now. "I'm Ivy Martin."

"Art Kimble. I own KBLZ. New radio station in town. I'd like to arrange an interview with Buddy on my show. He says you're the boss."

"Band manager. I'm sure we can work something out."

Strum slapped Buddy on the shoulder. "I'm outta here."

"Me too." Franklin called.

"Listen Ivy," Art said. "I told Buddy I would like to take you two to breakfast or something."

"I think I said to call me tomorrow." Buddy was trying hard to now to control his temper. He knew that if he didn't hold on, he would knock the man on the floor.

"How about you, Ivy?" Art persisted.

Buddy couldn't see the look Art was giving Ivy, but he knew the voice, recognized the invitation. This guy was severely pissing him off. He slid his arm around Ivy's waist and walked her away. "She has plans."

In the car, with Mojo sleeping in the back seat and Ivy driving, tension was as thick as the cigarette smoke had been in the club. A summer rain drummed against the windshield and roof as they moved through the dark streets.

"Don't do that again, Buddy," Ivy said.

"Do what?"

"Make me look like a mindless possession in front of someone."

"Guy was coming on to you, Ivy."

Ivy stopped for a traffic light and the rain intensified on the car's exterior. "I'm not a teenager. I can handle a guy flirting with me. This one could do us some good. You need to go on his radio show."

"I don't dig the guy and I don't want you alone with him."

"You made me manager. I'm going to call him and set it up." They were moving again. A brisk wind picked up the rain and rocked the vehicle. Inside, the car was silent except for the swoosh of water as the tires hit the pavement while they drove along the night streets.

"Buddy, let's not fight about this."

"No fight. I told the guy you handle all the business. I just don't dig the way he talked to you." He knew he was being unreasonable. "What's he look like?"

"I don't know. Tall, blond hair, kinda long. Looks about like he's late 30s or early 40s."

"Good looking?"

"I guess."

"Wearing a wedding ring?"

"I didn't notice. For God's sake Buddy, stop it."

He reached over and put his hand on her leg and she curled her fingers around his.

Chapter Twelve

The branches of two ancient live oak trees reached out and touched, giving shade to the backyard of Franklin's family. From the oil drum barrel cut in half to fashion a barbecue, the smell of spicy-flavored pork ribs filled the air. Buddy sat in a slatted lawn chair, holding a can of Dr. Pepper. Ivy, on the grass, leaned against his bare leg, one arm draped over his knees. Mojo slept curled up in a ball by the chair. Across the yard, he could hear the shouts of Franklin and his brothers playing touch football. He remembered when he was a kid, playing football in the park, running like hell with the ball hugged to him and hands pulling at him, trying to bring him down. Bet he could still do it today with Franklin and the boys, he thought. Just that little problem of not being able to look where he was going.

"You should see all the food on the table," Ivy said. "Rows of salads and desserts."

"What'd we bring?"

"A cake from the bakery."

They laughed together since Ivy never cooked anything for potlucks. Buddy put out his hand and stroked her hair. It was silky and warm from the sun filtering through the trees.

"I love summer," Ivy said. "Especially the fourth of July."

"Good thing it's on a weekday this year or we'd be working." Buddy ran his hand from the top of her head to the bottom of her hair, cut blunt and straight just below her shoulders. "We've been working a lot the last few months, thanks to you."

"Better clubs too." She squeezed his knee to emphasize her statement.

"Sure are." He tousled her hair. "Our CD's getting' a lot of airtime too. So, are we rich yet?"

"I've booked you for that KBLZ show Saturday morning." Her voice was serious now, the laughter gone from it. "Buddy, we need all the publicity we can get."

Buddy decided not to reply, remembering the argument they had the night they met Art Kimble, the owner of KBLZ, and how he came on to Ivy. Instead Buddy took a drink from the Dr. Pepper in his hand, wishing it was a beer. One brew was not going to send him on a journey, but Ivy would get anxious if he even mentioned it.

"Have you seen Rufus?" he asked

"No. Everyone else is here. Strum even brought his son."

"Rufus has a lot of attitude lately. Don't know what to do about it." Buddy tried to remember just when Rufus started snapping at everything, acting like a jerk most of the time.

"He doesn't like me being manager."

"I think it's more than that. Might have to let him go."

They were silent, listening to the chatter of conversations around them and the laughter of children playing. There was the clink of horseshoes hitting metal stakes and men cajoling each other along with the shouts from the football game. Above it all, he could hear Jimmy's voice across the yard, singing an Irish ballad. His rich tenor climbed into the air like the smoke from the grill and hung there before fading away. Buddy knew Franklin's father would be splashing sauce on the meat as several men around him gave advice on the best method of barbequing.

"Did you bring your guitar, sir?"

Buddy recognized the voice of Strum's son Tyler.

"Never leave home without it."

"Maybe you can show me how you do that one phrase like you do on your new song."

"You ask your daddy to show you?"

"He said ask you."

"You bring your guitar?"

"Yes sir. I'll go get it."

At a party like this, every musician was expected to bring his instrument, to jam a little before night ended. They loved it as much as the people who gathered around to listen.

"You want me to get yours?" Ivy asked.

"I think so."

Buddy felt Ivy stand up and move away. A breeze caught the live oak branches and they rustled overhead. The horseshoe game broke up as someone called "Ribs are ready!" The hum of conversation grew as people moved toward the food.

"Here you are, Buddy. Some ribs and coleslaw."

Buddy reached out for the paper plate Franklin handed him. He heard the young man flop down on the grass beside his chair just as Tyler returned with his guitar.

"Buddy's gonna show me how he does that one riff of his," Tyler said, banging his guitar a little as he pulled it from the case.

"Oh, you mean that part in *Last Call*?"

"That's it." Tyler handed his instrument to Buddy.

Buddy slid his fingers along the frets. "What's this, a Jackson?"

"Yeah. Christmas gift from daddy."

"Nice. Treat it right." Buddy cradled the instrument. "They got a place to plug this in?"

"Yeah, they ran a cord outside. One of those big kind with four slots Guess they expected us to need one."

Buddy began to play, the chords coming from his fingertips, fueled from somewhere inside a dark hole. He closed his eyes and went to that place where the music came from and found the riff Tyler was asking for.

"It's the thumb," Tyler exclaimed. "You're using your thumb!"

Franklin took a harmonica from his pocket and blew softly. The lonely sound drew pictures of campfires, riverboats, and jail cells. It called to the soul, Buddy believed, that inexpensive instrument, carried in the pocket of life's sojourners.

People gathered around the musicians, dragging chairs up, sitting or standing in the shade, the aroma of cooked ribs and potato salad floating on the breeze. It wasn't long before Strum's bass joined in, and a muted trombone added brass. The distinct style that defined Amos, came in over Buddy's shoulder and he could feel the guitarist rocking on his feet as he played. Someone in the audience, a woman with a powerful blues sound, started to sing about the *Birth of the Blues* and the musicians joined her, backing up the old, traditional tune. Buddy thought the singer was Lizzie Jones, lead gospel singer at the Church of the Nazarene.

When Ivy handed him the Gibson, Buddy gave Tyler his guitar and the young musician joined in with the others, taking a solo. Buddy stopped playing and listened with admiration at the young man's skill. He had known him since he was a child, trying to carry his daddy's guitar case around when Strum brought him to rehearsals. The impromptu band took a break while Buddy and Ivy teamed up to sing George Gershwin's "*There's a Boat That's Leaving for New York*" from the folk play *Porgy and Bess*. It was a song they had done many times alone at the piano in their condo. Someday, he thought, they might record it.

The night grew cooler and the sound of fireworks accented the music. A trumpet joined a bongo drum, and a second harmonica. Everyone sang *Won't You Come Home Bill Bailey*, clapping their hands and shouting at the end. Jimmy's strong voice lent an Irish brogue to the blues that made the Louisiana natives laugh.

Buddy smiled in his heart. He was alive with every note, every phrase. But, as the evening deepened, the sounds of fireworks disappeared, and the hum of bug zappers became active. People drifted away, rounding up children and calling good-bye. The trombone left, then the bongo drum and the trumpet. Ivy went to help clean up the table, and the music slowly faded away.

"Thank you, sir," Tyler said.

"You're going to be a hell of a musician," Buddy held out his hand. "You already are."

"I'll second that. I surly will." Rufus said.

"When'd you get here?' Buddy asked.

"A while ago."

"Glad you could make it. We got a road trip coming up in about a week. I wanted to tell you about it. I need to get my Winnebago ready to roll. It's still torn up from when it was vandalized."

"Yeah. Good, good. I can dig it. Listen man, I got a cousin does carpenter work. He can fix the RV up for you; get it ready to roll in a few days."

"Let's get him on it. We're all anxious to get going."

"Play the blues again in real blues clubs." Rufus laughed and slapped Buddy on the shoulder. "Ivy's not coming along, is she?"

Chapter Thirteen

Buddy listened to his own voice, low and raspy, floating over the speakers as he sang *Last Call*. Ivy was singing backup and the guitar had Amos' trademark sound as he took a solo at the end of the first frame, bending a note high on the guitar's neck. Ivy's hand on his arm felt warm and comfortable as the CD played on. They were quiet until the end, when Art said: "This is KBLZ in Baton Rouge. We're back with Buddy O'Brian and Ivy Martin. This is their new CD, climbing the charts, crossing over from blues to mainstream with the fans. Nice to have you both here in the studio."

"Fans call me Blind Buddy. You can too."

"We're happy to be here, Art," Ivy said. "We want to thank you for playing the new CD. We're pretty proud of it."

"I want to tell you, Buddy, that you are one lucky guitar player to have this woman. She's not just a terrific singer, but she's gorgeous too."

Buddy felt his body go stiff and Ivy's fingers tighten on his arm. He gritted his teeth and adjusted his dark glasses. "Yeah, I'm a pretty lucky guy there."

"I understand she is also the manager of your group, Mojo's Blues Band."

"That's right, she's the brains." He knew there was sarcasm in his voice.

"Where'd you come up with a name like Mojo's Blues Band for the group?"

"Named after my dog. Been with me since I was eighteen. Shake hands with the man, Mojo."

"Ladies and gentlemen, there's a big German Shepard here in the studio right beside Buddy. Just got up and shook my hand, but I don't think his heart was in it. That's some paw, there, 'bout the size of a saucer."

"Certified seeing-eye dog. Everybody knows I'm legally blind. Especially the fans."

"Then you don't know how good looking this woman is."

"This is the third time you've told me."

Ivy's hand was pinning him to the chair. She spoke up. "Buddy and I have known each other since we were in elementary school. Before the accident that damaged his eyes."

Buddy knew she was trying to keep him from losing his temper.

"You folks out there know what they call a guitar player without a girlfriend?" Art was speaking into the microphone now, talking to his audience. "Homeless." He laughed and then said, "You're on the air, caller."

Completely pissed over the homeless joke, Buddy was half way out of his chair and Mojo was on his feet when the caller's voice filled the room. Buddy recognized Eldon's whine.

"Finally got a CD out? Was you drunk or sober? That between your benders?"

"What's your name, caller?" Art asked.

"I'm the guy who brought this drunk off the street and gave him a career. But he fired me. Ask him if he ain't a drunk. It don't matter, even a blind squirrel gets an acorn now and then."

"Get hip to this, Eldon; you're not my manager anymore," Buddy snarled.

"Hear you sending your main squeeze around to get you gigs."

"Yeah. She does a damn good job. Keeps better books than you did, Eldon."

"What does that mean?" Eldon snarled.

Ivy was leaning over him, close to the microphone. "This is not the time or place, Eldon."

"Yeah, well like the old song says, I'll be suing you."

Buddy heard Art flip on the switch for music and the control room was quiet. In the distance, he could hear his voice, singing another track from the new CD.

"Wow." Art chuckled a little. "Some show."

"That was so ugly," Ivy said.

"Audience will eat it up. Looks like you had some bad feelings with your old manager."

"He cooked the books." Buddy didn't like talking about his problems with this disk jockey. "We'll take care of it in court."

"Called you an alcoholic," Art persisted. "That true?"

"I haven't had a drink in a week. How about you?" Buddy was holding back, remembering he was on the air. "You want to talk about music or not?"

"You're a pretty colorful character, aren't you, Buddy?"

"That's for other folks to say."

"Wait!" Ivy intervened. "Art, could we just stick to the CD? All this strife may be good radio but we're not going to hang around for it. What'll it be?"

"Whatever you say." Art was laughing now, that nervous kind of laugh people do when things have gone too far.

Buddy felt Ivy's fingers lace through his and he sat rigid in the chair. He'd have to swallow some pride here to make her happy. A cool glass of Jack Daniel over ice would help sooth him, calm this storm gathering inside. Hang on, he told himself as he heard his recorded voice, muffled as it played over the speakers.

Art flipped the switch. "You're on the air caller."

"Just want to say what a fan I am. Blind Buddy, you're the best damn blues guitar man since Stevie Ray Vaughan."

"Thanks, man."

"I'm digging this new CD. I'll be buying it."

The hour dragged on. Art made stupid jokes, chatted with Ivy, and took calls from fans. Buddy could visualize Jack Daniel's honey-colored liquid as it splashed over two ice cubes in a short glass. No mix, neat, with just the pure nectar that took away the pain; that took him to that dark place where he could hide from all the Art's and Eldon's in the world. He thought of placing the glass to his lips and letting the cool liquor roll over his tongue; of the sharp bite and smoothness as it went down to temporary fill the hole inside him. The wait for relief as it spread to the senses.

He answered the questions as callers continued to ask the same ones over and over. Yeah, he started playing when he was sixteen in the school for the blind. He played the piano before that, played it by ear; learned to read music at the school. Who inspired him? Well, he guessed it was those old guys like John Lee Hooker but he liked Eric Clapton and B.B. King. That's who he listens to now. Loved to play concerts alongside Red

Archibald. What a showman. His favorite of his own music? Well, that would be the latest one, *Last Call*.

Buddy answered them in his voice that was as deep and scratchy as a windy day. In his mind, he was pouring a measure of Jack into a squat glass and admiring the amber liquid when Art asked:

"What's your next gig?"

"Going back on the road for a while. Doing a concert in Nashville and a couple of clubs along the way." Buddy turned to Ivy. "Where you got us booked, baby?"

"We're doing two nights in Memphis and three in New Orleans."

"Come back and see us when you get home to Baton Rouge." Art stuck out his hand and Ivy pushed Buddy to take it. "Thanks for coming on the show today."

Art flipped up the volume as *Last Call* came over the speakers again. Thank God, it was over at last.

"Can I buy you two some lunch?" Art asked.

"No thanks." Buddy was firm.

"Another time, Art." Ivy was trying to make up for Buddy's rudeness.

"Anytime you're free," Art said

Buddy bristled at the double meaning there and added one of his own. "She's always free, man."

Ivy, Buddy, and Mojo walked down the hall and entered the elevator.

"Well, that went well," Ivy said as the elevator descended silently down to the basement parking garage. "First Eldon calls and then you insult the host."

"Told you I didn't like the guy." Buddy lowered his head and smiled.

Inside the car, Ivy said, "I'll drop you at home; I have some things to do."

"No, carry me to Jimmy's."

"Buddy—are you sure that's a good idea?"

"Ivy—I said take me to Jimmy's."

*

The bar was cool and the lights were dim. Benny Goodman's clarinet playing a swing tune came from the jukebox so Buddy knew the place was empty. He settled on a stool and Mojo dropped to the floor at his feet.

"How are ya, my boy?" Jimmy asked, that Irish lilt to his voice.

"Give me a shooter of Jack."

"Come on now, Buddy, you know—"

"Is Sam's Place still selling whiskey on the next corner?"

"You're not going to go do something crazy again, are ya?"

"I earned this one, Jimmy. Just give me a shooter."

Jimmy touched his wrist and slid a short glass in his hand. Buddy lifted it to his lips and let the magic liquid slide over his tongue.

Chapter Fourteen

The glass was empty. Buddy wanted another drink, but he knew where it would take him and this wasn't the time. One more and he would not stop until he was in the dark pit so deep that someone would have to drag him back again. He slid around on the stool and walked with measured steps to the upright piano, the path burned into his memory. He reached out to feel the sturdy familiarity of it, lowering himself onto the bench and opening the lid, touching the ivory with his fingertips.

"Remember that Cajun song Yvette liked so much?" he asked, running the keys lightly, finding the melody. "*Jole' Blon*, wasn't it?"

"Sure and it was. How she would dance!" Jimmy was standing beside the piano now.

Buddy played and remembered his mother dancing across the barroom floor without a partner. Her beauty and the grace of her movements would cause people to turn in their seats to watch, and the looks he saw in men's eyes were easy to read even though he was just a kid. As long as he played she would whirl and move, laughing with each step. She would stop, catching her breath, and hug him to her, calling him sweet names. She would whisper *mon petit chou*, her face against his, gin in her voice and on her breath. He could still smell her sandalwood perfume, remember the softness of her hair as it fell over him, and feel the layers of beads around her neck as they pressed against him. When she died, this was the memory he kept and he would never let it go.

Maybe he was crying now, he couldn't tell. But he was almost sure that Jimmy was. He finished the song and put his hands flat on the keys.

"You have the look of her," said Jimmy, "and none of me, even though you are my own son. But you have a wild Irish heart."

"Corn beef and cabbage tonight, Jimmy?" Change the subject while he could still control the need just below the surface.

"No, it's to be chicken and dumplings. Will you be staying now?"

"I'd like to stay all night, if it's okay."

"You're welcome, my boy." A hesitation and then, "Shall I call Ivy?"

"Let her know not to come after me. Tell her I don't want to talk right now."

After supper, people straggled in for a drink and conversation, not wanting to stay home when the summer evening was still light and warm. Most were regulars coming in, tired after a day's work, drinking beer, throwing darts and playing liar's dice. Buddy drank a beer and shook the cup, having others read the dice for him when they rolled out on the bar. When he won, he bought drinks for the house. He played the piano, taking requests from the customers, while Mojo slept at his feet. Sometimes, Buddy just felt the draw of this bar, his home. He was overcome with a desire to connect again with the boy he was before his life changed and threw him into a shadow world. He needed the love and acceptance he always found here.

When Jimmy finally locked the doors behind the last customer and wiped down the bar, Buddy slumped over the piano, abstractly finding snatches of old tunes to improvise on. Jimmy brought a chair over to sit beside him and sang old big band standards while Buddy found the chords by ear.

That night he slept in the bed of his youth, and in his dreams, Yvette danced and laughed on the barroom floor. The next morning, he called a taxi and left before Jimmy woke up. He had made it through the night and now it was time to go back to Ivy and the world they shared.

Ivy opened the door of the condo and he could hear the relief in her voice when she greeted him. "Why didn't you call? I would have picked you up."

"Hey, baby," he said and kissed her. "Got any coffee?"

"Sure. Some eggs too if you want."

"Let me get a shower first. Oh, could you feed Mojo?" Buddy freed the dog from his leash and listened as his toenails clicked across the floor beside Ivy who was crooning to him.

It was the game they played, he thought as he stood under the hot water in the shower stall, the warmth of it soaking into his skin. Ivy pretended to understand why he had to go home in his random way. But he knew she didn't. She was afraid when he took a drink, knowing it could lead to days of blackness and never knowing when the next time would be. Still, he was grateful for whatever kept her with him all these years.

In fresh jeans and a polo shirt, he padded barefoot into the kitchen to take the cup of hot coffee. Ivy slid it across the table to him and he was devouring the eggs and toast when she said, "We got a letter from Eldon's attorney. He's suing us for breach of contract."

"No surprise there."

"We'll have to get an attorney. I can find one through my old job."

"Good idea." Buddy pushed his plate away. "Better do it before we leave on tour. Is the RV ready to roll?"

"Rufus has his cousin working on it. Said it'll be ready on time."

"Where're we playing tonight?" Buddy ran his hands over his hair and tugged at the gold loop in his left ear.

"Blues Incorporated."

"One of the old clubs? Thought we stepped up."

"One night gig. We had a hole in the schedule. Rufus talked to the guy and called me with it, so I said okay just to keep him happy."

Mojo jumped to his feet just before a knock sounded on the front door. Ivy went to answer it. "Why, hello detective. What brings you by?"

Buddy was standing when Ivy said, "Buddy, its Detective John Allen from the Memphis police."

"You remember me, Mr. O'Brian?" It was the detective's even voice.

"Of course man, I never forget a face." Buddy put out his hand. "Anything wrong?"

"Still working on Jake Washington's murder. I believe it's connected to your singer's death someway. Could be wrong, I suppose." Allen shook Buddy's hand.

"Sit down and have some coffee with us, please," Ivy invited.

Buddy smiled. Ivy was ever the Southern hostess.

"You find a connection?" Buddy sat down again as Allen scraped back a chair and Ivy poured coffee.

"Nina was a user and Washington was a supplier. Both were murdered by experts. That's all I got so far." Allen settled in his chair. "No cream, just sugar. I just take my coffee black. Comes from all those night shifts I worked as a rookie."

Playing on the stereo in the bedroom, June Christy's voice floated in. That's the way Ivy liked her music, as if it were borne on a breeze. Jazz, unlike the blues, Buddy often commented, was not usually raw and in your face.

"I'm down here meeting with the detective on the Baton Rouge PD, seeing if we can put anything together," Allen went on, "and I got the idea to come by to see you. Maybe you'd remember something that would help."

"Nothing I can think of," Buddy sipped the cooling coffee.

"Nina a long time junkie?"

"For as long as I knew her. About six or seven years."

"Any idea who would want to see her gone?" Allen's cup clattered against its saucer. "Who her dealer was or anything like that?"

"I don't know who she was buying from. We didn't socialize after work."

"How about you, Ms. Martin?"

Ivy had been quiet all the time Allen was asking questions. The subject of Nina was a touchy one because of the time Buddy had been with her, snorting white powder, falling in the downward spiral. Even though Buddy had chosen Ivy, that had been a rough time in their relationship, almost tearing it apart.

"Nina and I were not friends," Ivy said with that edge in her voice.

"Well, you think of something, let me know. I'd like to clear this case." Allen rose and then stood there as if he forgot something. "By the way, that was a nasty exchange on the radio yesterday. Sounds like you got some real problems with your old manager."

"We'll handle it in court," Ivy said.

"Yeah." Allen was moving toward the door. "Like I told you before, I think you need to watch yourself, all the same. You still got my number?"

"I'll keep a look-out," Buddy said. "See ya later."

Allen was chuckling as he got up from the table. Before he reached the door, he stopped and said, "I'm serious. There's a killer out there."

Chapter Fifteen

Ivy ordered a tuna on wheat sandwich and a glass of sugared ice tea. The lunch hour was over and the crowd was gone from the Downtown Diner in the business district of Baton Rouge. It was a popular place for the office workers in the area and Ivy liked the motif of lots of glass, chrome and red vinyl. Ceiling fans with large blades whirled overhead, mostly for show because an air conditioner kept the small diner cool and customers lingered, dreading the heat outdoors.

It had been a busy morning for Ivy as she met with two booking agents and had another scheduled for the afternoon. Her hair was pulled back and caught with a ribbon and she wore a sleeveless blouse with a full skirt and wedge sandals. She hoped it was professional enough; it was too hot to dress otherwise. She was finding it stressful work to keep the band working, promote the new CD, and most of all, to keep Buddy from disappearing into some dark place for days.

Just as she reached into her large bag and pulled out her Blackberry to check her notes, a man's voice said, "Ivy Martin. Hello."

Art Kimble stood there looking expensively casual in a white shirt hanging loose over faded jeans that came from the designer that way, and white gym shoes. With his perfect tan and blond hair, he looked as if he should be carrying a tennis racket.

"Hello Art, nice to see you."

"You're as lovely as ever," he said. "May I sit down?"

"If you like. I'm just having some lunch before my next appointment."

A waitress placed a sandwich and a glass of tea in front of Ivy. "Can I get you something," she asked Art.

"I'll have a glass of tea. No sugar," he said.

"Not from the South, are you?" Ivy teased. "We drink our tea sweet down here."

"No, I'm from New York."

"You never said if you are married or have kids."

"No, not married," Art said. "Divorced. Got a boy, six years old now, lives in New York with his mother."

"Sorry," Ivy said.

Art shrugged. "She's an actress. Two egos collided I guess."

"You must miss your son."

"I get up to New York to see him often as I can."

"Shouldn't you be on the air?" Ivy asked, uncomfortable with the conversation and with the way his blue eyes never left hers.

"I have a later program," he said. "You must not listen to my show."

"Sorry, I keep my radio dial on KJAZ. Never turn it."

"That seems strange for someone who makes a living off the blues."

"Maybe," Ivy drank from her tea glass, "but I'm really a jazz singer. I'm just doing the new CD with Buddy."

"Aren't you touring with him too?" Art accepted a glass from the waitress.

"Just while promoting this CD, trying to get it going."

"Then you're going back to jazz?"

Art smiled and it irritated Ivy. "That's right. Why? Do you find that strange?"

"Someone classy like you," he said, "should be on stage with just a trio and a spotlight singing jazz like June Christy or Anita O'Day."

"Nice dream but not much call for that kind of singer anymore." She bit into her sandwich.

"What you need is someone like me to manage you." He leaned forward, "How about it? I can book you tomorrow."

For a moment he made her see it again; that dream she had since she was a kid, where she was singing jazz in a place where people listened and called for more. Maybe she'd have a flower in her hair like Billie Holiday or a teasing half smile like Peggy Lee.

"I have a repertoire and a pianist who accompanies me. Actually I've done most of the supper clubs around here," she said, feeling as if she should be defending herself. "I just put that on hold in order to promote this CD. I'll go back to it when we get Buddy and the band on top again."

"You'd be great in Miami Beach. I can see you now." He looked at her over the rim of his glass as he took a gulp of tea. "We'd make a great team. I've got the right contacts."

Ivy had to break loose of this image. My God! She thought, he's like Sportin' Life, the guy in Gershwin's *Porky and Bess*. The guy who lured Bess away from her true love and back into the wild, city life. Just like in the song she and Buddy sang together. This was the man who could seduce her away from her life and change it forever. The choice, she knew, was hers to make.

"Look," she said, changing the subject. "I want to say I'm sorry things did not go well when Buddy and I were on your show."

"I thought things went really well." He was chuckling at the memory. "It was pretty entertaining and got some good response afterward. I'd love for you both to come back."

"Glad you found it so amusing."

"It was fun," he said. "That guy who called in, his former manager, what's his name? Dubois? He said Buddy is a drunk, is that true?"

"What a rude thing to ask. Of course it's not true. It's just sometimes when the pressure gets too much for him, he becomes depressed and he needs to be alone to work through it. Creative people are like that."

"He's lucky you're so understanding."

Was that a note of sarcasm in his voice? She'd heard it for years, all those well meaning friends, co-workers and relatives telling her she should leave Buddy. This man certainly didn't know her well enough to go there.

Ivy put her Blackberry away and took her wallet from her bag.

"Let me get this," Art said.

"No thanks," Ivy pulled a bill from her wallet and placed it on the table. "I need to go. I have an appointment."

"Let me buy you lunch tomorrow. I can meet you here at one," Art said, rising as she did.

"Sorry, can't make it," Ivy said, gathering her things.

"I really want to see you again," Art said.

Chapter Sixteen

Buddy and Amos returned to the room behind the stage where early in the evening they had taken off their suit jackets and draped them over the back of a chair. There was no air conditioning in the small dressing room, or anywhere else in the old building where Blues Incorporated was located. The blades of a table fan whirled, but they were little help in the humid night heat. A door opened to an adjoining toilet and seeking a cool surface, Mojo retreated there to lie on the tile floor.

"Thought we'd seen the last of these dives," Amos said. Something about his voice always seemed to have a smile in it.

"Rufus booked it. He likes these places."

"That boy never gonna get any class. You needing a ride?"

"Yeah, Ivy went on home early. The heat got her down." Buddy thought it more likely the bad elements of the bar crowd had driven her away. From the stage, he had smelled the body sweat and alcohol and marijuana rising from the dance floor. There was the shrill laugh from a drunken woman at the bar, louder than the rest. The constant cigarette smoke, rumble of voices and moving feet surrounded him. The night and the band played on for a whiskey-soaked crowd, wet with perspiration. Now, at closing time, laughter faded into the dark as people reluctantly found their way out of the nightclub doors.

"Where's that dog?" A man's voice came from the dressing room entry.

"He's here. In the bathroom." Buddy answered. "Who wants to know?"

"Virgil Simpson, club manager. Looking for that woman takes care your business."

"Talk to me," Buddy said.

"I want to pay you. I need to get going."

"I'll take it." Buddy put out his hand.

"Lock that dog up first. I ain't coming in with him there."

Buddy reached over, felt for the bathroom door and pulled it shut. "Come on in."

"I'll go get the car." Amos moved to leave but Buddy grabbed his arm.

"Hold it, man. I want you to do the count."

Virgil Simpson called the bills as he placed them into Buddy's hand. Amos counted with him. "That's cool."

"You guys were grooving tonight," Virgil said. "Bought one of your CDs myself."

"Thanks." Buddy rolled the money into a ball and put it in his pants pocket. "See you another time."

"I'll bring the car around," Amos said. "Franklin and Strum already gone."

After Virgil and Amos left, Buddy moved across the room, wiped his guitar down and put it in his traveling case. It had been a hard night with sweat running down his face and he guessed the band members' too. There were only osculating fans pushing the hot air around the fetid building while they played and the crowd danced. Next week they would perform in an air conditioned concert hall in Nashville. Ivy was doing a good job of getting them into better places and included in group concerts.

A shadow moved in the doorway and Buddy turned to face it. "Back already, Amos?"

The shadow moved toward him without answering. Buddy called out to Mojo, remembering too late the dog was shut up in the bathroom. Buddy moved slowly in that direction. Mojo began barking and throwing his weight against the closed door.

"Just give me the money," the shadow demanded. "Or I'll kill you."

Buddy inched toward the bathroom door, where Mojo was lunging and snarling on the other side. The shadow moved along with Buddy, growing larger, closer; closing the gap between them, one arm extended. The weapon must be in his right hand, Buddy guessed as he backed against the bathroom door. In a moment he would be close enough.

"Just drop the money on the floor," the voice was whispering, a nervous edge to it. "Don't want to hurt no blind guy. Shut that dog up."

"Sure. It's cool, man," Buddy said, inching backward along the wall, not sure what was in the shadow's hand; could be a gun. "Here's the money, right here in my pants pocket."

Buddy put his hand in his pocket and slipped the knife out, springing the blade free. The shadow lunged and something made contact with Buddy's face just as he leaned sideways. Buddy slashed with the knife, felt it rip flesh. A scream of pain and a curse came from the assailant. Buddy twisted the door knob to release a leaping Mojo into the room. A shout punched the air. Footsteps, followed by Mojo's snarl, echoed down the hall, receding in the distance. Worrying that Mojo could be hurt, Buddy called to him.

"Mojo!" Buddy whistled, dropping to his knees. "Mojo! Come here, boy! Heel!"

Relief rushed through Buddy as he felt the dog's wet nose nuzzling him. Buddy hugged the hairy animal. If the guy had a gun, he might have killed Mojo and Buddy wasn't sure if he could live with that.

"What the hell? You okay?" Amos came sprinting in, out of breath. "What happened? Some guy with blood all over him almost knocked me down in the hall."

"Anybody catch him?" Buddy asked.

"No, he was running like the devil had him," Amos was catching his breath now. " Mojo on his heels."

"You chase him?" Buddy stood up, one hand still holding onto Mojo. "Was it that manager?"

"No, I never saw him before. You bleeding on the side of your face. Probably should have it looked at. Want me to call the police?"

"Just drive me on home," Buddy put his pocket handkerchief up to his face, flinching as it pressed against his wound. A deep throb was beginning in his head. "I don't want to be here all night."

"He get the money?"

"No. Mojo saved it." Buddy patted the dog's head.

"What the hell's going on in here? Jesus! Look at your face." Clayton, the bartender came in the room.

Buddy could feel the handkerchief he was holding to his face was becoming saturated with blood. The wet feel and smell of it was repugnant and he needed to get home and get a dressing on the cut before it dripped all over his clothes.

"Some guy came blowing through the place and out the door," Clayton went on, "Jim, my bouncer went after him. But he lost him in the dark. He mug you?"

"He didn't get anything for his trouble but a cut-up arm," Buddy said.

"I'm calling the cops."

"Do what you have to, Clayton." Buddy picked up his guitar case. "I'm going on home. They need to talk to me, that's where I'll be. Let's go Amos."

"I'll get fired if I don't report it."

"You know where I stay."

"Damn," Clayton grumbled, "I'll be here the rest of the night with this. Virgil left me to close up."

Buddy didn't talk on the way to Ivy's place. Neither did Amos. They'd played low-life skid row bars and honkytonks most of their working lives. They had been assaulted before in the black hours of closing when ordinary folks were safe in their beds. Still, it left a deep grudge inside and an anger that stayed with Buddy in the daylight.

"Least he didn't get the money." Amos said.

"Yeah."

"What the hell's going on, Buddy?" Amos said, the smile missing from his voice. "First Jake's murdered, then Nina. Now this."

"That's life." Buddy shrugged, the cut on his face throbbing. Detective Allen said those same words to him this morning.

Chapter Seventeen

It must have been three in the morning by the time Amos walked in the front door with Buddy and said good-night. Ivy, wakened by Mojo, came out in the hall and took Buddy's hand.

"My God, what happened?" she asked. "There's blood running down your face."

She led him into the bathroom, and as he explained, she examined the wound.

"Some guy tried to mug me. Mojo ran him off."

He grimaced as she washed the cut on the side of his face and put a square of gauze against it, securing it in place with surgical tape.

"It really needs stitches," she said as she placed two aspirin in his hand and waited until he put them in his mouth before giving him a glass of water to chase them down.

"What's one more scar?"

"He could have killed you," she said.

"He didn't."

"You think he was just after the money?"

"What else?" He pulled off his shirt, dropped it on the floor, and walked past her to the bedroom, kicking off his loafers and falling across the bed.

Her voice followed. "I don't know. It just seems that so much is happening."

"Give it a rest, Ivy. It's the kind of world we live in, you know that." Buddy was very tired and his head throbbed. He needed a visit from his friend Jack Daniels. He could almost feel it now, tossing the liquid down neat, with a sweet bite as he swallowed.

Now as he lay on the bed, she crawled up beside him, kissed his bare shoulder, and ran the flat of her hand over the dark hair on his chest. She laid her head in the crook of his arm and he felt the warm comfort of her nearness. The silk of her hair and the scent of her perfume should have aroused him. But he put his arm over his eyes and did not respond to her, choosing instead sleep and its dark dreams.

Ivy went out early the next morning and Buddy was alone when the doorbell rang. Mojo barked once and ran across the floor. Barefoot, wearing jeans and a T-shirt, Buddy put down his guitar and went to the door.

"Yeah?"

"Police," came the answer.

Holding Mojo back, Buddy opened the door. The shadow told him it was a woman, about medium height. Her voice was firm and she introduced herself as Detective Carolyn Harper of the Baton Rouge Police Department.

"I understand you were attacked last night."

"They don't usually send a detective to take a report on a mugging, do they?" Buddy asked, motioning her inside. He followed her shadow as she came in and sat on a straight back chair. He perched on the sofa arm and Mojo settled down at his feet.

"John Allen from the Memphis PD is a good friend," she said. "He asked me to come by if you ever had any trouble. He's concerned about you."

"He's a good man, but he doesn't have to worry."

"Maybe not. But tell me what happened, anyway."

Buddy told the story, leaving out the part about his knife and the slash on the guy's arm. They didn't need to know he carried an illegal switchblade.

"Mojo gets all the credit," he said, patting the dog's head.

"You think it was a setup?" she asked. "That the manager was his partner?"

"I believe anything's possible."

"This ever happen to you before?"

Buddy turned his head toward the kitchen and pursed his lips. He waited a moment before turning back, and then said, "In my line of work, shit happens. Especially if you're blind."

They were silent for a minute, and then Detective Harper said, "Your voice is just like it is when you sing."

"How's that?"

"Kind of like you have a sore throat or something." He heard her move in the chair. "I'm sorry; I don't mean to be rude. That was really a compliment."

"You a blues fan?"

"Actually, not really. John Allen played your CD for me. He's a big fan."

"You his girl?"

"We're friends." The chair creaked as she moved again.

"Next time we play Baton Rouge, come to the show as my guest."

"I'm not sure that would be permitted. Department regulations and all."

Buddy smiled. "The offer stands if you can work it out. You and Allen."

"Look, we'll talk to this Virgil, the club manager," she said, back to business. "He'll deny everything, naturally. You think of anything else, let us know."

Detective Harper rose and moved toward the door. Buddy got up and walked behind her, wanting to see her out, remembering his manners as a southern man. She stopped abruptly and turned, bumping into him. For a moment, they were face to face, their bodies touching, and Buddy could feel her strength of presence, the lack of feminine softness. She was not wearing perfume, but there was a faint essence of fresh soap. He thought she must have the body of an athlete, and hair cut close to her head. He'd felt the hard budge of a gun under her light blazer.

Stepping back, she said, "I'm so sorry. I just wanted to leave my card with you in case you need to call."

"Lay it on the table by the door."

"Yes, of course." She seemed nervous. "Well, good-bye then."

"Tell John Allen I'm okay, and thanks for his concern."

"Yes, I will."

"We're leaving on tour tomorrow, doing some dates in Tennessee. Maybe I'll see him when we get to Memphis."

"I'll let him know."

She was gone, shutting the door softly behind her. Buddy smiled, standing in the middle of the floor, the soap smell still in the room. He was attracted to the strength of Detective Carolyn Harper, and how she became flustered as a teen-age girl when he was suddenly in her comfort zone. It was like the women who came backstage after a gig, not knowing what to say once they got his attention. Maybe he'd never meet Carolyn Harper again, but he put her down in his mental black book.

"Who was that?" Ivy came in the front door. "The woman who just left here?"

"One of my lovers." Buddy laughed at the silence that followed. "Just kidding. She's Baton Rouge Police. Friend of Detective Allen."

"About last night?" Ivy came to him and touched the bandage on his face.

"Yeah."

"Nice looking for a cop."

"What'd she look like?"

"Dark hair, short. Kinda pretty and a body like she works out."

"She's Allen's girl." Buddy sat down on the sofa and picked up his guitar.

Ivy was walking down the hall to the bedroom. Over her shoulder, she called "Winnebago's ready. We can leave in the morning."

Chapter Eighteen

The scent of gardenia came closer and Buddy reached out to touch Ivy's bare shoulder. He ran his hand along her collar bone to her neck, touched the dangle of her earring and tangled his fingers in her hair.

"What're you wearing?" he asked.

"Just a little black dress with thin straps across the shoulders."

"You look like a million bucks."

"How would you know?" Her voice had a smile in it.

Buddy pulled her to him and ran his hand down the silk of her hair. "I know," he said in her ear.

"Later," she promised. "We need to get to the club now."

"Look out the window and see if the RV is back."

She moved away and then said across the motel room, "Not there."

"We'll have to get a taxi to the club."

"Buddy, I asked you not to let Rufus take the RV today. Where'd he go anyway?"

"Said he had friends here in Memphis he wanted to see. Way he's been acting lately, I just wanted to smooth things out some. He got some attitude about us not playing Aunt Martha's this trip."

There was hostility and anger in the way Ivy grabbed the phone, ordered a taxi, and threw the receiver back in the cradle.

"We are through playing places like Aunt Martha's," she said. "This show tonight with three headliners will put us back in the game. He'd better make it in time to play."

Buddy hoped so too, but he didn't say anything. He picked up his guitar and called to Mojo. Ivy laid his suit jacket over his arm and they walked out of the room to the elevator. Strum, Amos, and Franklin met them in the lobby. There was the hum of voices, cars stopping to unload, and the fresh smell of rain and wet earth as the doors opened and closed.

"We'll see you at the gig," Strum said. "We'll take the van."

"Know where Rufus is?" Buddy asked.

"No, but we got his drums. He'll show up."

"This is a big night," Ivy said. "Two other top bands."

"Yeah." Amos said. "We'll out blues 'em."

"You look mighty pretty, Ivy."

"Thank you, Franklin. Let's hope I sing pretty."

"Never heard you sing any other way."

"Taxi's here, Miss," the bell captain called to Ivy.

Buddy remembered the streets of Memphis, with its mixture old and new, prosperity and poverty. Tonight they were wet with a light summer shower that that hissed under the tires and Buddy could hear the rain tapping on the windows of the taxi and the windshield wipers as they whisked across the glass. By now the lights would be bright against the dark evening and he could make out their glow as they flashed off and on.

"My goodness," exclaimed Ivy, "there's a line outside the club. Driver, take us around back."

"Like a rock star?" Buddy quipped. "We're blues musicians, Ivy."

He felt her lean forward to give the driver money; heard her say, "Keep it."

They got out of the car, Buddy slinging the guitar case over his shoulder and Mojo brushing against his leg. Ivy took his arm and they walked into the building toward the noise and music.

The Blues Journeymen were already on stage, the harmonica matching the guitar note for note. The entire club seemed to be rocking with the sounds of roadhouse music. Buddy felt an excitement, a thrill of the moment that was like coming home.

"Buddy," Ivy touched his shoulder. "Here's Matt Mitchell."

A hand clasped his, slapped his shoulder. "How ya doing, brother?"

"Hey, Matt. Good to see you."

There was the chuckle that always came when he said that. The shadowy mountain of a man that was the leader of the Blues Lifters leaned toward him, his breath near Buddy's face.

"You too, man. What's the line-up? You up next or us?"

"You're next, Matt," Ivy said. "A very hard act to follow."

"You guys are pretty hot right now with that new album and all," Mitchell said. He reached down to pat Mojo on the head. "Still got the group leader here, I see."

"It's Mojo's Blues Band. I just play the guitar."

The Blues Journeymen were bringing it in, rolling to a close amid whistles and applause from the crowd.

"Gotta go," Mitchell walked away.

"Ivy," Buddy asked, "Are the guys here?"

"All but Rufus."

"Got an hour before we go on. He'll show." Buddy hoped he sounded confident.

"You want to sit out here or in the band room?" Ivy asked.

"Band room would be fine."

In the small room filled with stale air, Buddy could hear the thunder of the crowd when Matt Mitchell and the Blues Lifters were introduced. He could hear the hard beat of the drums and the three guitars coming together behind Mitchell's harmonica. Then Mitchell was singing *Sweet Home Chicago* and the music was bouncing around in Buddy's brain. God! How he loved it! It never grew old.

"I'm going to the ladies room," Ivy patted him on the arm. "Be back in a minute."

As she left, Buddy reached for the table he knew was beside the chair where he sat. He moved his hand slowly across the table top until it touched a bottle. He smiled, thinking there is always one in a musician's room. Picking it up, he unscrewed the bottle's cap and there was that unmistakable aroma. He put the bottle to his lips, tilting it up. The bourbon came into his mouth, sweet and biting. He gulped a long pull, savoring the burn as it went down. Recapping the bottle, he put it back on the table just as he heard footsteps.

"We up next?"

"Where you been, Rufus?"

Rufus laughed. "They left you alone with a fifth of whiskey? What were they thinking?"

Rufus put a round plastic container in Buddy's hand. "Breath mints."

Buddy ran his fingers over the plastic until he found the lip of the lid. He flipped it open with his thumb, took two round tablets and put them in his mouth. Hot cinnamon. He snapped the container shut and tossed it back toward Rufus' voice.

Mojo stirred and a voice said, "Hope it's okay if we come in."

"John Allen." Buddy got to his feet and extended his hand. "I'm glad you came."

The fresh soap smell he remembered from the other day came closer. "Carolyn. You came after all."

"I have a couple of days off so I came to Memphis. John said we needed to hear you. He's a big fan."

Buddy took her hand in his and squeezed it gently until she pulled away. "I hope you will be too."

"I'll convert her." There was affection and some possession in John's voice.

"Oh, this is my drummer, Rufus Coleman. Rufus, this is John Allen of the Shelby County Sheriff's Department and Carolyn Harper of the Baton Rouge police."

"Do we get arrested if we play bad?"

"No, we're just here to enjoy what you do."

"I invited them," Buddy said. "They're my guests tonight."

"Nice to meet you," Rufus mumbled. "I got to set up. Enjoy the show."

They were silent as Rufus left the room. There had been quiet hostility in the drummer's voice. Buddy knew it was a dislike for law enforcement in general. Then Ivy came in and everyone was at ease again, shaking hands and making plans to meet for a late supper after the show.

"It might be pretty late," Ivy said. "We don't know the city that well."

"There's an all night diner over on 24th Street called Mandy's," said Allen. "I worked the C shift as a patrolman so I got to know all the late haunts."

"I know the place," Buddy agreed. "Use to go there after a gig every time we played Memphis."

Then Franklin's voice in the doorway, saying, "Martin's finishing up. Get ready."

The bottle of whiskey on table called to Buddy. Only a couple of feet away. A thousand miles. He reached out to the place he had left it, but his hand grabbed only air. Ivy must have spotted it.

"John, you two take a seat out front." Buddy picked up his guitar, lifting it out of its case. "Ivy, tell the manager to get them a good table and put their drinks on my tab."

Franklin took Buddy's arm. They walked to the edge of the stage just out of sight of the audience and Franklin left Buddy there, holding his guitar and Mojo at his side. An announcer was asking everyone if they were having a good time and people were responding with whistles and applause. They quieted down and he raised his voice to say "Give it up for Blind Buddy and Mojo's Blues Band."

Already on stage, the band began the opening song, a Texas roadhouse blues number that rocked the place. Toward the end of it, Ivy took Buddy's arm and led him onstage to the front of the band. The audience went wild with applause and shouts as he took his place, Mojo dropping full length at his feet. He adjusted his guitar strap around his neck, and as soon as it was quiet enough, reached for the microphone and said in his raspy voice, "This one's for you, Carolyn."

He gave a downbeat and they swung into *Trying to Cry You Back Home.*

Later that night, when the four of them were seated at Mandy's Diner drinking sugared ice tea and eating shrimp sandwiches, Buddy hoped Ivy and John Allen didn't notice when his hand brushed against Carolyn's or how her voice changed when she spoke to him, taking on a different quality, like a woman flirting with someone she just met.

"Thank you for the song," Carolyn said.

"You're welcome. I hope you liked it."

"I think we're winning her over," Allen said in that friendly way of his.

"The blues is like Tangueray gin, you acquire a taste for it," Ivy joined in. "I didn't care for the blues at first either. I still prefer jazz, but Buddy is a bluesman. It's his life so I guess it's mine too. At least right now."

Buddy wondered what that meant.

"Lot of people confuse the two," Allen said. "Think they're the same."

"Lot of people are musically illiterate," Buddy said. "They mix up blues, jazz, rock and roll, even folk. Roll 'em all up in the same ball."

"All American made, I guess," Allen said, trying to defend the general public's musical taste.

"Blues has a rich history," Ivy said. "Some historians say it was the first original American music. Came up from the cotton fields, traveling the Mississippi to New Orleans and on to Chicago. It was the inspiration for rock and roll, and even before then, jazz, I guess."

Buddy knew that was not a concession Ivy liked to make. She could be a little bit of a snob when it came to jazz.

"Billie Holiday and Janice Joplin were really blues singers even though they were not billed as such," Buddy reminded her. "Billie was jazz and Janice was rock and roll, but if you listen to them, they're pure blues."

"Actually," Ivy injected, "Janice started out singing blues down in her home town of Port Arthur, Texas."

Carolyn was silent during the discussion, but Buddy felt her leg move against his and then away, as if it were an accident. But it had lingered a little too long for that.

"Do you mind being called Blind Buddy?" Allen asked, his glass of tea clanking against his plate.

"There was Blind William Jefferson, Blind Blake and Blind Willie McTell, all blues pioneers during the 1920s," Buddy said. "I'm proud to be associated with them even though I don't play the same style blues."

"What about you, John?" Ivy asked. "Buddy was born to be a musician, but did you always want to be a police officer?"

"I guess so," John seemed reluctant to talk about himself. "Long as I can remember, I wanted to help people, never liked to see them treated unjustly. I did a hitch in the Marines, got out and joined the Memphis PD. It seemed right. Still does."

"You too, Carolyn?" Buddy said.

"I'm not the nurturer John is," Carolyn answered. "My motives are not so pure. I like a challenge."

Buddy smiled and his leg accidentally touched hers.

Chapter Nineteen

Ivy was asleep, pressed against Buddy, her breath even and steady against his chest. He held her, feeling her body damp and warm in the afterglow of lovemaking. He had told her he loved her. Said it over and over like the lyrics of an old song, one he knew so well he never had to think of the words as he sang, meaning them all the same. Still, the very familiarity of them was a distraction from their sincerity.

He kissed her forehead and smoothed her hair, then rolled over. She moved with him and clung to his back, throwing her arm around his waist. The need to be free from her grasp rose inside him.

He disengaged from her, sliding his legs over the side of the bed and sitting up, hesitating as the mattress sighed under his weight. He got up, found his way to the bathroom, and turned the shower head on full force. Stepping beneath it, he let the pounding water run over him until it turned icy cold.

They were in Nashville, the last stop on their tour, playing the ballroom of a big hotel. As part of the contract, management had given them rooms with upscale accommodations. It was one of those things Ivy did so well, negotiating terms beyond money.

They slept late into the afternoon. Franklin came by and took Mojo for a walk. Ivy ordered room service for her and Buddy and the two of them ate dinner with the television turned to an all-news station. After a while, there was a knock on the door and Buddy heard Franklin moving into the room, talking to Ivy.

"Mojo had his walk and dinner, so he's fine now."

"Thanks for doing that, Franklin," Ivy said.

"I don't mind. Not much else to do."

"They take care of the sound check?" Buddy asked.

"Doing it now. Strum is with them."

"Rufus set up?"

"Some hot looking babe in a caddy picked him up several hours ago. He's not back yet. Amos brought the drums in."

"Damn him," Ivy said. "He's got the key to the RV. Said he left his suit in the closet and needed to get it out."

"No. He gave the key to me after he brought his suit in. Got it right here." A ring of metal hit the table top.

"He better be back in time to work."

"Let it go, Ivy, he's never missed a gig yet." Buddy was growing weary of the tension between Ivy and Rufus.

"I'll go on down and help with the sound." The door clicked shut behind Franklin.

There was a hard silence in the room. Buddy petted Mojo and waited, knowing Ivy wanted to argue over Rufus. Instead she said, "I'm going to take a shower and get ready."

At eight o'clock Buddy went down to make sure things were ready for the show. Rufus came in just as they were finishing the sound check, a woman with a tall shadow and a brassy laugh came with him. Rufus introduced her as Ruby.

"You the one they call Blind Buddy," she said in a voice a little too loud. "I heard you play before, and I got all Rufus' CDs."

Buddy did not reply, wondering where Ivy had gone off to.

"Sorry to hear about your singer," the voice went on, "I liked her style. One you got now, not enough soul."

"Let's get a shooter, baby," Rufus was laughing, leading her away.

Ivy came up, asked Strum to get the show started. She stood backstage with Buddy until the band opened with a number that grabbed the audience's attention right away. Amos took the mike and welcomed the crowd, asking them to put their hands together for Blind Buddy and the Mojo's Blues Band.

Waiting behind the curtain, Buddy, wearing a black shirt, black leather jacket and a black porkpie hat, adjusted his sunglasses, ran his forefinger down the scar on his face, and tugged slightly at the gold loop in his ear. The fans liked him to wear sunglasses on stage, he wasn't sure why, but it sometimes helped if the spotlight glare was too bright on his damaged eyes. When he walked on stage with Ivy and Mojo, there was loud applause, but no whistling or stomping, telling him the crowd was older, more sophisticated. In this city where country music was king, there were still some blues lovers.

As soon as they reached the microphone, Ivy started into *House of the Rising Sun* and he sang harmony with her. Amos took the guitar lead and Franklin played a wailing harmonica for the sad story of degradation and despair. This was how Buddy liked it with Ivy, sharing the music with her, melting their talents together the way they had since they were fifteen-year-old kids in Spanish Town. He kissed her at the end of the song and the audience liked that too. She left the stage and the band settled into serious jump blues until the first break.

There was no band room, so the musicians went outside during break. Franklin led Buddy through a side door that opened to the back near a parking lot. It was quiet except for an occasional car motor starting. The night air was heavy with humidity, but smelt clean after a light rain shower. A sudden breeze cooled Buddy and dried the sweat that gathered on his body from the heat of the crowd and the bright spotlight focused on him when he was performing.

"Strum here?" Buddy asked.

"Yeah, I'm here."

"Get me a beer, will ya?"

"You sure?"

"Yeah."

"You want one too, kid?"

"Yeah," Franklin answered. "I'll wait here with Buddy."

Buddy heard the door shut behind Strum. He was quiet for a moment, then, "Be home tomorrow night."

"That's good. I'm missing everybody," Franklin said. "My daddy's probably needing me to help on his new building job."

"When I get home, I'm going to take Jimmy fishing. Just him and me and Mojo out there on the river."

"Not Ivy?"

"Naw, she don't fish."

"Here you go." Strum placed a bottle in Buddy's hand. It was cold and wet against his palm. Putting it to his lips, he swallowed half the liquid, the carbonated brew drowning his thirst. But it was a poor substitute for a shot of Jack Daniels.

"You see Rufus?"

"Sitting at the bar with his new squeeze. Woman's a looker. She's hot, man."

"Round him up, let's get back on stage."

Just before the end of the show, Ivy returned to the stage and sang one of the new songs from the CD. Buddy sang *She's Funny That Way* in a sun-going-down style that ended the night. They broke into *Trying to Cry You Back Home,* and when it was over, he stood at the front of the stage and talked to the people, signing a bold BB with a black marker pen on CD covers for the crush of fans that thrust them into his hands.

When they were in their hotel room again, Buddy kicked off his shoes and dropped his leather jacket on the chair he bumped into. Ivy called for room service.

"Get me something with sea food," Buddy said. "And a glass of white wine."

He felt her hesitate, and felt the resentment rise inside him as he waited for her rebuke.

"Just one. Need to relax." He wanted to yell that what he really wanted was a fifth of Jack, that he was not a child, didn't need to be managed or disciplined. He felt his nerves unraveling to a ragged edge.

Ivy drew her breath as if holding back. He knew she wanted to argue about the wine but she picked up the phone and gave the food order, asking for two glasses and a bottle of Chardonnay.

She backed up to Buddy. "Unzip me."

He pulled the zipper down and ran the flat of his hand across her back, smooth and firm under his palm. Leaning forward, he moved her hair aside and kissed the curve of her neck, the scent of her perfume almost as if it were part of her skin, belonging to her alone.

She moved away and turned to face him. "Buddy, when we get home you have to fire Rufus."

"No."

"Don't you see how he's doing? How he's acting?"

"I said no, Ivy. It's still my band."

Buddy went into the bathroom and turned on the shower.

Chapter Twenty

The willow tree Buddy sat under gave respite from the hard sun overhead. Out on the lake, water birds called to each other. He leaned back in the canvas folding chair, put a harmonica to his lips and blew a few cords of *Up the Lazy River*.

"Don't be scaring the fish away now," Jimmy said.

"You catch anything yet?" Buddy could hear the high whine of the reel as it released fishing line being cast wide and far into the lake.

"They will bite when the wee people tell them to."

"Well whisper to the wee people that we need a couple for supper tonight."

Buddy was wearing a T-shirt, shorts and flip-flops. A straw pork-pie hat was perched on his head above his dark glasses. August in Louisiana is merciless, clutching the land in heat and humidity like a wet fist. But the willow branches hung down as if to protect him, insects hummed by and an occasional breeze gave relief. He loved the South and its people, its history, the feel of its culture, and, most of all, its music.

His mind drifting, he remembered the feel of Carolyn's hand as he squeezed it in his a few nights ago in Memphis. Imagination took him on a tour of the rest of her body and he indulged himself in the thought of spending exploring minutes, even hours, with her. Women, he had found, always want the man who makes music and find it hard to separate the musician from the person. But with Carolyn, who didn't even like the blues, the connection was more than that. It was an electric current that ran between them each time they met.

"The fish are hiding from the heat," Jimmy called from the water's edge. "I'm going to take a swim."

"Be careful of cottonmouths," Buddy answered. "Bound to be some snakes in that water."

"I'll take Mojo in with me. He needs to cool off too."

"Go on Mojo," Buddy said to the panting dog lying on the ground beside him. "Take a dip with Jimmy."

The splash as Jimmy hit the water and Mojo barking with excitement brought a smile to Buddy lips, but the familiar resentment welled up behind it. In the old days, when he could see, he would have swung out over the lake on a rope and dropped into its depth. Boys from the neighborhood would dunk each other under the water and race to shore. Now, he swam only in pools with someone to point the way to its concrete sides.

Rising from his chair, Buddy unfolded his cane and made his way back to the motor home. He switched on the radio, set on the Baton Rouge station, KBLZ. B.B. King and his unmistakable guitar style came over the speakers. Buddy stopped to listen to the characteristic phrases used by the blues master, high on the register, holding the sound and settling into a steady rhythm. The song ended and Art Kimble's voice came on. It was that fake tone he used on the air, so controlled and friendly. Off the mike, he spoke rapidly, his voice was higher and thinner.

"King of the blues, there," he said. "Now I want you to listen to one of the best women singers to come along in a long, long time. Miss Ivy Martin, a beautiful lady with a beautiful voice. Here she is with Blind Buddy and the Mojo Blues Band singing *Suppertime* from their new CD.

Buddy clutched the cane so hard he thought it might break. He punched the back of the passenger seat and swore loud enough for his words to carry outside to the peaceful silence of the lake. That son-of-a-bitch was still after Ivy, making her the focus of the CD as if he and the band was just her backup group.

He went to the cabinets and threw open the doors, his hands searching the contents. There must be a fifth of Jack Daniels hidden there somewhere. He kneeled down to the bottom cabinets, reaching in, touching each object, his fingers over flying every container; cans and jars falling over or against each other. Like a starving prisoner, he was frantic in his search to fill the need in the pit of his stomach, in the hollow place in his mind.

Out of anger, he banged his fist against the bottom cabinet and the plywood gave way. Reaching inside, his hands found a container about the size of a shoebox. He pulled it out, fumbled with the lid and lifted it, running his hands over the contents. A large block of something was wrapped in plastic. He found the opening and peeled back the covering.

What the hell?

He wet his finger and ran it across the block, and then put the finger to his mouth. There it was, the unforgettable taste on his tongue, as familiar as if he had sniffed it just yesterday. Cocaine. It was a full brick of uncut cocaine, worth a small fortune on the streets of Baton Rouge.

Buddy slapped the lid back on the box as if it contained one of the cottonmouth snakes he had just warned Jimmy about. He had been down into that white pit before and it had almost swallowed him whole. He was more afraid of it than he was any man with a weapon.

On the floor with the box in his lap, he felt sweat break out on his forehead and under his arms. If the police found something like this in his possession it could be the end of his career, no doubt prison time. Ivy and Jimmy would leave him for sure. No one would believe it wasn't his. But who hid it there, thinking no one would find it under a fake bottom?

He was conscious of Mojo barking in play as Jimmy called to the dog, urging him on. Buddy began to put things back in order, straightening up the cabinets. He put everything in place, except for the shoebox. Couldn't leave it there for Jimmy or someone else to find.

In the near distance he heard Mojo barking and Jimmy laughing, coming nearer. Buddy picked the box and carried it into the bedroom, shoving it into the bottom of his duffle bag, packing clothes on top of it. If Jimmy saw it, he would never believe it wasn't Buddy's.

"Don't shake that water all over me," Jimmy was on the step, talking to Mojo. "Let me get on some pants and I'll fix us all some supper."

They ate outside in canvas chairs, in the coolness of evening, with day fading to night, birds settling into trees, and nocturnal creatures waking to search for food. Jimmy served up his Mulligan stew with big chunks of bread from the bakery down the street from his pub. Buddy drank a Dr. Pepper, gritting his teeth against the need for a shot of Jack.

As it grew later and the crickets and frogs began to sing, Jimmy started to hum.

"Can you use your mouth harp now to play some good old Benny Goodman tunes?"

Buddy pulled the harmonica from his pocket and blew *Memories of You*, soft and low. He knew it was the song Jimmy wanted to hear, thinking of Yvette. Jimmy was silent, not singing along as he often did. The lonely music floated up into the night.

But while Buddy played, his mind repeated again and again the feel of the brick, the taste of white grains against his tongue. Cocaine. Temptation pulled at him, but he knew one sniff would set him back on the shadowy road to hell.

The devil drug would not let him alone. Even as they played cards, the edges Brailed, at the table inside the motor home, music soft over the radio, and Jimmy laughing, Buddy's tongue felt the hexing promise of cocaine. When they said goodnight, he tossed in bed, involuntarily turning toward the duffle bag and the block of sorcery hidden there.

How did it get into his RV and who would be coming back for it?

Chapter Twenty-One

"It's John Allen," the voice on the other side of the door said.

Mojo squirmed beside Buddy as he opened the door of the condo and John Allen stepped inside.

"Thanks for coming on short notice, man," Buddy said, reaching out to shake the detective's hand. "You made it from Memphis in record time."

He took the hand with a firm grip. "Left as soon as you called."

"Figured you'd be the best one to turn to."

"What's the problem?" Allen closed the door behind him.

"It's all coming down just like you said." Buddy felt a sense of relief now that he could share the problem of his discovery in the motor home. It felt good to be sharing it with a police detective who would believe him when he heard the story.

"What happened?"

"How about we sit down?"

Ivy's voice floated in from the bedroom where the radio stayed tuned to KBLZ.

"They playing your new album?"

"Yeah, they give that number with Ivy a lot of airtime." Buddy wanted to be proud but the old resentment lay just below the surface. Like Ivy was the star here and he was just a band leader. "It's climbing on the charts."

Sunlight streaked the floor through open drapes and fell across the men as they walked into the living room. Buddy sat in the overstuffed chair and motioned Allen to the sofa. This whole mess had Buddy feeling like he was in quicksand, being pulled under, inch by inch. He leaned forward to talk to the detective.

"Someone stashed two bricks of coke in my RV. Found it a couple of days ago when I went fishing with Jimmy."

Allen whistled low. "Where was it?"

"Fake bottom in the cabinet."

"Secret compartment could have been put in when they repaired the damage from the break-in." Allen's voice was calm, like he was considering the possibilities. "Who did the work?"

"Relative of my drummer, Rufus." Buddy reached up and touched the gold loop in his ear and then ran his fingers through his short curls. Closing his eyes, he realized that the person behind this was someone close to him and it was a fact he didn't want to believe.

Allen was cautious in his conclusion. "The dope could have been put there while you were in Memphis or somewhere else on your tour. Who has keys to the motor home?"

"Rufus drives it, sometimes Franklin." Buddy hesitated, and then added, "And Ivy."

"Any of them could have put it there or had a key made."

"Listen, John, I want you to take the dope. Get it out of my house."

"You got it here?"

"Yeah. I can't afford to get busted with it. So, you got to take it."

"You know they'll come looking for it."

Buddy knew they would. Knew they wouldn't let that kind of money go. Just a matter of time before they found it gone. Maybe they had already.

"I'm hurtin' either way," he said.

"What about Ivy?"

"She doesn't know I found it or that I called you and she's not going to."

Allen got up and moved around the room, Mojo stirred on the floor beside Buddy's chair. From the distance Etta James' husky voice sang a love song.

"You know I have no authority here," Allen said. "I need to call Carolyn."

"No way around that?" Buddy didn't want her to know about his life and all the dark places he lived. It was strange that it mattered to him but for some reason he wanted her to think of him in a positive light, not the rogue blues player image that often characterized him.

"No." Allen stopped pacing. "We need a plan. Get Carolyn in on it because it's her jurisdiction."

"Do have to say I gave it to you?"

"Well—maybe not. I'll figure it out."

"I'll talk to Ivy, find a reason for her to leave town until this is worked out. No need to tell her anything." Buddy was still not sure she would believe him even if he did tell her.

"Give me the stuff and I'll take it with me."

"In the other room. I'll get it."

As Buddy walked into the bedroom to retrieve the box, he heard Allen talking on his cell phone, saying he was coming right over to the station, that it was important. Buddy found the duffle bag, pulled the clothes out and threw them on the floor. He reached in and touched the box as if it was a bomb that could explode if he handled it wrong. He carried the gym bag into the living room.

"That it?" Allen said.

Buddy sat the bag on the table and opened it. He opened lid of the box and the bricks lay side by side, wrapped in clear plastic.

"Uncut." Buddy said. "Straight from the source."

Allen gave out another low whistle."You were right to call," he said. "This is a pile of money waiting to be made."

"Can you keep my name out of it when you take it to the station?" Buddy asked. "Don't need to be pulled in for questioning. Might make the news."

"Do what I can. I gotta go now." Allen walked to the door with the whisper of the nylon bag rubbing against his jeans. "Take care. You need protection."

"I got Mojo."

"He's not bulletproof and neither are you." Allen opened the door and the sultry heat came in from the summer day.

"What are you going to do?" Buddy felt relief that the bag was leaving. With the cocaine out of the house, its insistent pull was gone and the danger becoming a user again diminished. He had resisted the white siren call but how much longer he could have held out was uncertain.

Allen took Buddy's hand and placed a card in it. "My personal cell number is on here. Have Ivy put it in your speed dial or memorize it. Or do both."

"What should I do meanwhile?"

"Sit tight and wait," Allen said. "Someone will come looking for you. Be ready to call if its not one of us."

＊＊

Buddy was feeling a little less nervous by the time Ivy came home. She came in the door with the smell of Italian spices floating around her.

"I got us a pizza," she called out. "Are you as hungry as I am?"

"Pretty much," he answered as she kissed him on the check.

"Settle down in the living room and we'll eat in there," she said.

They ate three-cheese pizza and drank Dr. Pepper, sitting on the floor and using the coffee table to dine on. Music came from the bedroom, jazz on a summer afternoon.

"Ivy," Buddy said, "I want to play New York. We've never done that."

"Well, I don't know. I guess there are a lot of blues clubs there."

"Not just the clubs." Buddy reached over to stroke her hair. "I want to play Carnegie Hall."

"Wow!" She reached up and took his hand. "That's a big leap. I don't know who to contact for that. Probably have to plan a year out."

He took a chance, hoping it would work. "Other blues groups have played there and I know we're good enough. Go up there and see whoever it is you have to see."

"What? You want to go to New York?"

"Not me, Ivy. You go. Take your sister Jan and stay a few days. Maybe she can get some quick tickets on that airline she works for."

"What's this about?" Suspicion in her voice.

"The thing is, baby, I really want to play Carnegie. Also, we've been together night and day since the tour began. We both need a break."

"I can't leave you alone." He felt the air move as she moved her hand in a dismissal gesture.

He took her hand between both of his and kissed her fingers. "I've got Mojo and the guys from the band if I need help. There's some songs I want to work on and you know I do that better when no one is around."

"I don't know, Buddy."

Even though her voice was full of doubt, he knew she would go, was thinking it over and seeing herself on the most important stage in America. Ivy had always been ambitious; had always seen her name in lights one day. He liked that about her.

"Carnegie Hall, baby," he urged.

"Would you be okay?"

"Go call Jan. Set it up."

Ivy reached for the phone and in a few minutes she and Jan were laughing, excitement in Ivy's voice. By afternoon she was packing, talking to Buddy as she opened drawers and pulled things from the closet.

"Jan got us two standby tickets on tomorrow's red-eye flight." Ivy opened a drawer releasing the sent of lavender from the sachet packets she kept there. "Maybe we can get tickets to a Broadway show while we're there. At least one off Broadway."

Mojo followed her back and forth, as if he knew she was leaving. Buddy sat on the bed and put his hand in her open suitcase. He touched the satin of a nightgown folded there.

"What color is this, Ivy?"

"Peach."

"I don't remember you having anything like this."

"It's new. Do you like it?"

"I'd like you to wear it for me."

She leaned over and kissed him lightly. "When I come home."

He grabbed her wrist and pulled her down on the bed.

Chapter Twenty-Two

Buddy's hand searched the surface of the night stand, fumbling across the crystal clock, knocking it over. He found the telephone receiver and pulled it to his ear.

"Yeah?"

"Buddy? This is Carolyn Hunter, from the Baton Rouge Police?"

"Carolyn." He dragged himself to a sitting position.

"It's about your dad, Jimmy O'Brian."

"Jimmy. What about him?" Maybe he was still asleep. Why would the police be calling about his dad?

"Is Ivy with you?"

"She's in New York. What about Jimmy?"

Carolyn hesitated. "He's in the hospital. Been beat up pretty bad."

"He's been what? What hospital? I'll be right there."

"He's in Mercy. I'll come by and pick you up in twenty minutes." The phone clicked and the dial tone came on, but Buddy still held the receiver to his ear as if waiting to wake up again and have it be a dream.

Beat up. Who would hurt Jimmy? Someone trying to rob the bar. Some druggie looking for a fast dollar. But he knew better. It had to be connected to the cocaine. Jimmy had been beat up and it had to be Buddy's fault somehow. Maybe he should have left the stuff in the hiding place. They would have come for it and nothing would have happened to Jimmy.

He brushed his teeth and ran his hand over the stubble on his face but didn't bother to shave. He just took a shower, pulled on jeans, a polo shirt, and stuffed his feet into loafers.

Punching the speed dial, he waited for Jason, the college student who lived two doors down to pick up his phone. Mojo rubbed against Buddy's leg as if sensing that something was wrong.

"Hullo?' A sleepy Jason answered.

"It's Buddy. Can you come and take Mojo for a run? I have to go out."

"Yeah. Be right down."

Probably up late last night, Buddy thought. Jason was a good kid who took Mojo for a run in the park every day in exchange for guitar lessons once a week. The guy didn't have any natural talent, but he worked hard at learning technique.

Pacing the floor, Buddy wondered where the hell Carolyn was. When the doorbell finally rang, he put his hand on the lock and asked, "Who's there."

"Carolyn Hunter, Buddy."

He opened the door and heard Jason calling to Mojo.

"Go on, boy," Buddy said, and the dog ran along the walkway. "Keep him until I get home, will you Jason? Don't know how long I'll be gone."

"Sure thing, Buddy." Jason yelled from a distance, then, "Come on Mojo. Let's go big guy."

Mojo was barking and his toenails tapped against the sidewalk as he ran to Jason.

Buddy stepped outside, shut the door behind him, and unfolded the white cane. "Thanks for coming Carolyn. Now, tell me what happened."

"In the car," she said, taking his arm. "I'll give you all I know about it."

Carolyn was a careful driver, moving through the city in such a slow, methodical pace that Buddy wanted yell at her to hurry. He waited for her to tell him what happened as they passed the neighborhood bakery with the smell of fresh bread floating in the air and the fire station that sent a truck wailing down the street. After what seemed like several miles later, Carolyn spoke.

"One of the regulars at the bar called the police," she said. "He stopped by on his way to work this morning, found Jimmy on the floor of the bar and called 911. Ambulance took your dad to the hospital. I saw the police report and called you."

"How bad is it?" A vision of Jimmy lying on the cold floor all night, hurt and bleeding brought anger boiling up inside Buddy.

"The doctor said he'll recover." Her voice was calm; a police officer talking to the relative of a victim. "He has some broken ribs and deep bruises."

Buddy reached up to pull on the loop in his ear; the gold was smooth and solid in his fingers. "Jimmy didn't have this coming."

Carolyn covered his hand with hers, "I know about the cocaine."

Her touch was firm and he liked her fingers over his, her palm over the top of his hand. "Jimmy didn't even know I found it."

"They must have thought he took it." Carolyn moved her hand away and he could tell by the way the car slowed and turned that they were at the hospital. She stopped, cut the motor, and set the brake. "I'll take you up. It'll be easier that way."

They didn't speak on the elevator or as they walked through the hall to Jimmy's room. Carolyn pulled the curtain aside, plastic rings scraping against a metal rod. There was the soft hum of the machine monitoring vital signs, the smell of antiseptic, and the shadowy mound of a body lying there. Right then, Buddy was almost glad he couldn't see.

"Jimmy?" Buddy slid his hand along the side of the bed, following the feel of cool sheets, until he felt a hand. "Daddy?"

"He's asleep now," said a voice Buddy did not recognize. "He has a morphine drip so he may be out a while."

"Who are you?"

"Valerie. I'm his nurse."

"How bad is he?"

"I'll let the doctor talk to you about that. Looks like he's going to make it though."

"Bring a chair over here will you, Valerie. I'll be here until he wakes up. Can I get some coffee?"

"I'll go down to the coffee shop and get you a cup." Carolyn touched his shoulder. "I'll be back in a few minutes."

Buddy sat in the chair listening to the muted voices in the hall; nurses going about their business, slipping from one room, one patient, to another. There was the low rumble of carts being pushed down the hall, the rattle of dishes as breakfast was delivered or cleared away.

A male voice behind Buddy said. "I'm Doctor Abrams. You his son?"

Buddy stood up and put out his hand. "Buddy O'Brian."

"You're the blues singer, right?"

"That's right."

"Big fan, myself. Been to your concerts here in Baton Rouge."

When they shook hands the doctor's palm seemed soft against Buddy's. He thought the doctor to be a tall man with a quiet voice.

"Thank you. How's my dad?"

"Well, they did a real number on him. Three broken ribs, fractured jaw, two black eyes, and a concussion." The doctor paused and Buddy suspected he was reading the chart. "Bruised kidney and liver. But, he'll be alright. We'll keep him here a few days and watch him. Right now, he's pretty uncomfortable."

"I'm going to sit here with him until he wakes up," Buddy said. "Thanks for taking care of him."

"No problem." His voice faded toward the door. "By the way, if I bring in your CD, I can I get you to sign it?"

"Be my pleasure."

After he left, Buddy put his hand on Jimmy's face, running his fingers across Jimmy's skin, touching gaze and bandages beside his brow, feeling swelling that must have closed his eyes. This laughing, singing Irishman, so generous in his emotions and his strength was here because Buddy was who he was. Jimmy was always so proud of him, even in the darkest of days, and this was his payment for that.

"I'll take care it Jimmy," Buddy said, leaning close to his ear. "I won't let this go."

Carolyn came back with a carton of coffee. She placed it in Buddy's hand and said, "It's got a sip lid on it. I got you a muffin too. I'll put it right here on the tray."

"Thanks, that's good of you," he said, taking a short drink of coffee and feeling a little better from the heat and strength of it.

"I'm going back to the office now," she moved closer to Buddy, "I'll come back as soon as I can and take you home."

"I can call Strum or Amos." He reached out and put his hand on her face.

"I'll come back," she said, her voice low, intimate.

Buddy felt the familiar thrill of treading on dangerous ground.

Chapter Twenty-Three

Only the muffled noises of hospital staff outside the room broke the silence as Buddy sat next to the bed, his hand covering Jimmy's. After a while, Buddy began to recall bits and pieces of random songs he remembered from years of listening to the big bands of Glenn Miller and Benny Goodman when he was a child. He began to hum, and then sang the songs in a low, husky voice that lent itself better to the blues than swing. But it was the music he knew Jimmy loved, and maybe, somewhere inside that morphine induced sleep, he could hear Buddy's voice and know he was there. In the middle of Duke Ellington's *Satin Doll* the hand under Buddy's moved.

"Buddy?"

"I'm here Jimmy." Buddy got to his feet and leaned toward the voice he barely recognized as his father's.

"Thank the saints you're alright." It came out tight, halting.

"What happened Jimmy?"

"Three men, they thought I had something that belonged to them." Jimmy spoke through clenched teeth, a wire holding his jaw shut. "Said they would get it from you. What is it, me boy, that they would do this for it?"

"Someone hid cocaine in the motor home, Jimmy. I took it out and gave it to the police. I should have told you about it but I didn't think they would come after you."

Jimmy moved his hand from beneath Buddy's. His silence cut Buddy through like a machete.

"I had nothing to do with the drugs, Jimmy. You have to believe me. They were using me and the RV because I can't see. They believed it must have been you took the coke because I'm blind and they wouldn't think I could find it."

Jimmy's unbroken silence hung in the air like an accusation. Buddy knew there was no reason that Jimmy should believe him, but he felt desperate to make him understand.

"There is a false bottom in the cabinet where they hid it. I accidentally found it." Buddy hated the pleading whine he heard in his voice. "I gave it to the police. I never touched it. I want you know I'm clean now. I'm so sorry they did this to you. I don't know who they are."

Buddy slumped down on the chair again. Footsteps and low voices of the hospital staff continued outside the door, but the room was quiet with unspoken anger and disappointment. For what seemed like a very long time, the silence held and Buddy wanted to cry in despair, not knowing how to convince his father he had no part in the drugs.

"He woke up, I see." Carolyn was standing behind Buddy's chair. "I'm Carolyn Hunter, Mr. O'Brian, from the Baton Rouge Police. When you feel up to it, we can talk about what happened."

Met with silence, Carolyn continued, "Your son has been very concerned about you."

"Can't talk now," Jimmy said, his voice slipping, growing faint and slurring, giving in to the morphine.

"I can come back. You rest and maybe I can take Buddy to lunch."

"You can carry me home," Buddy said, standing up and unfolding the cane.

"If that's what you want." Carolyn took his arm and they left the room without a word. It was not until they walked to the elevator and out of the hospital that they spoke again.

"He didn't believe me." Buddy said after he was in the car.

Carolyn backed the car out of the parking space. "I'll go back later. Maybe I can make him understand."

"I don't blame him. I've messed up so many times."

"Not this time, though." Carolyn pulled out onto the main street, where the sound of heavy afternoon traffic surrounded them. There was the loud exhaust of a bus pulling away from the curb, the sharp screech of brakes and a car honking.

"You don't really know, Carolyn, the trouble I've been to him or how many times I've disappointed him since Yvette died."

"Don't take this on yourself, Buddy. You did the right thing."

It wasn't a long ride and inside the cruiser the only noise was the intermitted crack of the police scanner and flat voices relaying messages, using numbers to communicate what was happening on the streets of Baton Rouge.

"I'll go in with you," Carolyn said when she parked the car at Buddy's complex.

Inside the condo, music drifted from the bedroom, jazz from the twenty-four station the radio stayed turned to. The smell of Ivy's perfume was faint but noticeable as Buddy and Carolyn walked into the living room. It was as if Ivy was there, waiting.

"Ivy's in New York?" Carolyn asked. "When's she coming home?"

"Next week, maybe." Buddy could feel Carolyn's discomfort with Ivy's invisible presence.

"You sure you don't want some lunch?" Carolyn asked. "I can make a sandwich if you have something."

She started to walk past him, but Buddy reached out and took her arm. She moved close to him and he touched her face, moving his fingers along her jaw line to where her chin came to a gentle point, across a straight, small nose and cheekbones that stood out as if sculptured. He kissed lips thinner than his full ones but drew the heat of response as she pressed against him.

His lips left hers and slid to her neck, tasting the smoothness there, the aroma of soap and freshly shampooed hair.

"You are the sexiest man I have ever known," she whispered.

He ran his hand over her hair and down her shoulder and arm, feeling her shiver. The phone rang, but he continued his journey along her body. She pushed back from him.

"You should answer that," she said.

"No." He put his hands on her shoulders and pulled her to him.

"It might be the hospital," she urged.

He walked to the desk and picked up the receiver. A voice as familiar as his own came over the phone. He smiled as he heard Ivy say; "Buddy?"

"Hey, baby, how's New York?"

"It's wonderful, darling," Ivy said. "And guess what? I meet with the booking agent for Carnegie Hall day after tomorrow!"

"I knew you could do it."

As Buddy stood there with the phone to his ear he heard the door to the condo open and close behind Carolyn.

Chapter Twenty-Four

"Also, I've got a couple of appointments today with some people to book two clubs here in New York," Ivy said.

"That's my girl."

"Jan went to visit with some of her airline friends that are stationed here in the city. No sense in her tagging along with me."

"Be careful going around alone."

"I'll take taxis everywhere, don't worry. Oh, there's someone at the door."

The sharp rap came a second time, filling the hotel room.

"I'd better see who it is. I'll call you later Buddy."

"Who is it?"

"I don't know, honey, I'd better see. I'll call you after while."

Ivy snapped the cell phone shut. She was sitting cross-legged on the burgundy and white stripped bedspread that matched the drapes on the windows of her hotel room. She uncrossed her legs and walked barefoot across the carpet to the door.

"Who is it?"

"Art Kimble."

Ivy opened the door and he stood there, looking as he always did; as if he had just come from the tennis court. His red polo shirt was hanging loose over pressed khakis and white Converse low cut tennis shoes. His even tan showed off his blond hair and the blue of his eyes.

"Art. How'd you know I was here?" Ivy was surprised and even a little startled to see him.

"It took some detective work, but I found you." He smiled. "Can I come in?"

Ivy was uneasy at the sight of him and the thought of bringing him into her hotel room. She knew he was interested in her, he had been flirting since the beginning. "I'm on my way out."

"Barefoot?"

"No. I just have to slip my sandals on." Ivy turned back into the room and he followed.

She searched the floor, finding the shoes in a corner where she had tossed them. She slipped them on, one foot at a time, standing up and leaning against the bed for support.

She smoothed the white cotton slacks she was wearing with a light yellow camp shirt and turned to face Art. "What did you want to see me about?"

"I don't remember," he said. "Just looking at you takes my breath away."

"Then inhale deeply because I'm on my way to a couple of appointments."

She moved to walk toward the door but he stepped in front of her.

"Ivy, have a drink with me," he said. "Down in the bar. Lots of people around."

"Art, I have to meet with some booking agents about business." Ivy reached for her purse, picked up the room key card and slipped it inside. She gathered up a small portfolio and stuck it under her arm. "Drinking beforehand is not a good idea."

"How about later then, maybe dinner? They have a good restaurant here in the hotel. Or I could take you some place really nice if you want."

Ivy looked at him. He was handsome and charming in that Great Gatsby kind of way, so different from the earthy world of blues musicians and the moody, guarded emotions of Buddy.

"I'm here with my sister," she said, wanting him to know she was not alone. "We're sharing this room."

"Bring her along. I just want to talk."

It wouldn't be smart, Ivy reasoned, to alienate the owner of the largest blues radio station in Baton Rouge. Besides it was only dinner and Jan would be with them.

"We'll meet you in the hotel cocktail lounge at seven," she said.

**

The day did not go well. It was difficult to hail taxis on the crowded, heat-baked streets of New York. The steaming humidity caused her shirt to cling to her body and her hair was hot and wet against her neck.

The first agent was not there when she showed up for their appointment, leaving her waiting in an empty office next to the bar where several day drinkers sat. The walls were lined with framed and autographed black and white photographs of blues musicians who had played the club. They smiled, sitting behind drums, at pianos, held guitars, harmonicas or horns, and wrote personal messages to the owner as if they were old friends. Ivy knew many of the musicians in the pictures; Buddy had played gigs with them over the years. It was really a small community, the blues world.

After she had waited forty minutes, the bartender, a young man dressed in a shirt with the bar name embossed across the left pocket, came in to apologize and ask if she wanted something to drink.

"Don't know what keeping him, he's usually here by this time," he said.

Ivy refused the drink and handed the bartender a card. "Tell him I had to leave, but he can reach me on my cell phone. I'll be in New York for a couple more days."

Back on the sweltering sidewalk, she searched for a cab in the unrelenting traffic that filled the street. When one finally pulled over to the curb, she settled into the back seat, feeling relief in the chill of the air conditioner. She handed an address to the driver.

"You sure you got the right place?" he asked. "Not the best part of town."

"I'm sure."

The club was south of forty second street, near the water, and when they stopped at the curb, Ivy handed the fare across the seat.

"Want me to wait?" the cabbie asked.

"No, I might be a while. Thanks anyway."

She left the bright heat to enter the cool dimness of the blues club. She squinted until her eyes grew use to the dark. The place was almost empty, with a long bar down one side, cocktail tables in the middle and a small stage up front with a drum set and microphone ready for the evening. This time the owner was waiting for her. He was a short, overweight man with thinning hair. He seemed disinterested but polite.

"Milt Steinberg," he said, sticking out his hand.

"Ivy Martin. We spoke on the phone. It's very nice to meet you."

"Have a seat," Milt said.

They sat at a small table near the bar.

"Get you a drink?" he asked.

"I'd like a glass of water. It's really hot out there."

He motioned to the bartender. "Benny. Glass of water here."

Ivy opened the portfolio and placed Buddy's photograph on the table along with a sheet of biographical information. In the glossy eight by ten, an unsmiling Buddy cradled a guitar; his face was turned slightly so it showed his hair curling just above his shirt collar. His black porkpie hat was pushed back on his head and dark glasses covered his eyes. Milt took a pair of reading glasses from his shirt pocket, placed them half way up his nose, and studied the picture.

"Blind Buddy O'Brian. Don't he have a drug problem?"

"At one time, yes. But not anymore. He's been working steady for the last couple of years and has a new CD out. One of the songs is climbing on the charts right now, you probably have heard it, *Last Call*?" Ivy slid a copy of the CD across the table. "I'll leave this for you."

Benny brought a glass of water and placed it in front of Ivy. She took a deep drink, waiting for Milt to glance over the material she gave him.

Milt looked at her over the rim of his glasses. "You part of the deal?"

"I sing, yes." Ivy decided to be candid. "The band's been touring the south mostly. We've never played New York and we would really like to give it a chance because I feel certain they will like our style here."

"You guarantee he'll show up and be sober? Sign a contract with a clause to that effect?"

"We only work with contracts and you can add that in." Ivy returned his stare, feeling the pressure to keep Buddy under control. "You won't be sorry, he has a great new sound."

"Well," Milt said. "Let's talk price."

"We're asking three thousand for one night only. Your choice of Friday or Saturday."

Milt removed his glasses. "Little steep, isn't it?"

"Moody James gets five thousand. We think we're a bargain at three." Ivy sipped from the water glass. "We're a five piece group with a recognized name and a song climbing the charts."

"I can give you twenty-five for a Saturday night." Milt picked up Buddy's photo. "Got one of these of you?"

An hour later, Ivy left the club satisfied with the deal she had just reached with Milt. The afternoon heat assaulted her when she stepped out onto the sidewalk with traffic crowding the street, steam gushing from buses and pedestrians rushing past her. She whistled and waved her arm at a passing taxi and it pulled to the curb. I'm getting the hang of this,

Ivy thought as she jumped in, it's simply a different mentality than in the south.

As soon as she reached the hotel room, she peeled off her clothes and took a long shower, letting the water sooth her as she lifted her face to it and let it run through her hair. When, at last, she'd had enough, Ivy wrapped herself in a towel and fell across the bed.

When she woke the room was dark and she knew it was late. Jan wasn't back yet and they were due to meet Art at seven. She sat up and turned on the lights, wondering where her sister was. Better get dressed anyway, she'll show up soon, Ivy thought.

She pulled on an azure silk sheath dress with thin shoulder straps. The dress clung to her body and moved with her. She fastened large silver loops in her ears and a thin silver bangle on her wrist. Strappy high heel sandals and a thin stole completed her outfit. Almost seven and still no Jan. Ivy flipped open her cell phone and pushed her sister's number.

"Where are you?" she asked when Jan answered.

"I was waiting to call you when everything was settled. There's a party at Rachel's place, I'll give you the address so you can catch a cab and come on over."

"I made plans for us to meet someone for dinner," Ivy said.

"Who?"

"A business contact." Ivy was all at once reluctant to say it was Art.

"Cancel and come on to the party. Tell them you'll meet them tomorrow."

Pure Jan, Ivy thought, always living in the moment. Another time, Ivy might have gone to the party on short notice, but she realized she did not want to cancel this dinner with Art, and that realization worried her.

"No," she said. "You go on to the party and have a good time. I'll see you when you get in."

"It'll be late."

Most likely sometime tomorrow, Ivy thought, and that meant she would be alone all night with no Jan to run interference for her with Art.

"See you then. Have fun," Ivy said and flipped the phone shut.

Art was sitting at the bar nursing a cocktail when Ivy came into the hotel lounge. He stood up and waved to her, smiling as she came toward him. He was dressed in a light weight suit with a white shirt opened at the neck. There were those extra touches of a white handkerchief in the breast pocket of his jacket, a gold chain bracelet on his wrist and tassels on his loafers that gave him the look of someone on the page of a magazine.

He reached out and took Ivy's hand. "You're beautiful."

Ivy smiled. "Thank you."

"Shall we move to a table? What would you like to drink?"

"White wine. And a table would be nice."

They sat in a tuffed leather booth with green potted plants surrounding it. Art leaned forward as he spoke, the scent of his cologne soft and expensive. People walked past with an air of sophistication, dressed in evening clothes and talking in a quiet manner.

"Where would you like to eat?" Art asked. "I know some great places in New York."

Ivy heard the warning bells in her head, the voice that said be careful, watch where this is leading because she liked it too much. It felt glamorous and easy with someone telling her she was beautiful and making feel as if she were. Someone who was actually seeing her as he said it.

"Let's just eat here," she said. "I'm actually starving. I haven't eaten since this morning."

He held her arm as they took the elevator several stories up to the hotel rooftop restaurant. It was a steak house with small lanterns on the tables, painting of horses on the walls and a panoramic view of the city, dark now except for neon lights shining like stars. She ordered shrimp and he had a steak; called for the wine list and selected something from California. Ivy knew she was having too good of a time but she wanted it to go on.

They talked of nonessential things such as movies they liked best, books they had read and cities, even countries, they had visited. Ivy felt guilty because she was glad Jan was not there with them.

When they left the restaurant, she knew she should say goodnight and go back to the room. But when she started to say so, Art interrupted her.

"Please," he said, "let me buy you a cognac in the lounge."

She protested, "It late and I don't usually drink this much."

"Just one," he urged.

"Just one," she agreed.

Then, back in the leather seat, one cognac became two and they danced to the music of a trio playing pop tunes. Art led her on the dance floor in short, close steps and she felt a dangerous thrill growing inside her. He brushed his lips in her hair and tighten his hand around hers, pulling her nearer to him. The chemistry between them could not be denied and at the moment, she didn't want to deny it.

Ivy was sixteen when she became Buddy's girl and she had been with him ever since. He was the only lover she had ever known. It seemed to her that she had spent her life waiting for him. She waited while he was in the school for the blind; waited all the time he searched for a place in the blues world; waited while he wandered in a haze of cocaine with Nina. Now she waited for the success she knew was due him and through him, her. But tonight, she was like a school girl on a date and she liked it more than she ever imagined. But she wasn't a school girl and the man who held her close was no inexperienced boy.

"Ivy," Art said in her ear as they danced, "I can get you those bookings you're trying for."

"No. I can do it."

"I can make Carnegie Hall happen. I just have to make a phone call. I'd do it for you, Ivy."

"I can make it on my own." She stopped dancing and looked at him.

"Let me help you," he said. "You know how I feel about you. I think you feel the same way I do. There's something between us and we need to see where it goes."

"Art, I'm in love with Buddy. I always have been." Ivy walked back to the table and picked up her stole and purse. "I'm not cheating on him."

Art followed her. "He's a drunk, Ivy, a musician like a million others with an uncertain future. I can give you more; make you a star if that's what you want. You have the looks and the talent to be somebody on your own. Come with me, this is the world you belong in, not the shabby blues scene. That's all he can ever give you."

"You don't understand. He needs me."

Ivy pulled free, crossed the floor and left the lounge.

Chapter Twenty-Five

The band swung into *Trying to Cry You Back Home*. Amos took a long solo, experimenting with some creative riffs that made Buddy laugh with appreciation. It was a relaxed night and they were having a little fun, feeling comfortable in this small pub where they played so often. The Backstreet Pub was situated in a strip mall on the edge of an upscale development and it closed up early on week nights. The band was finished at midnight and customers wandered on home for that early morning work alarm.

"Anybody got to get on home?" Strum asked. "I'm going over to that after hours place in Spanish Town. Told those guys I'd come and sit in."

"I'm down with it," Amos said. "Can you wait for me until Caprice gets clocked out so she can go with us?"

"That the little blond waitress you been comin' on to all night?"

"That's the one. Maybe we can get something to eat at that Mexican place next to the club."

"Come with me, Buddy. Check out my new ride," urged Franklin. "First brand new car I ever owned."

"Carpenter business must be good," said Strum, "you can afford a fancy sports car like that."

"We're doing okay."

Buddy reached out for Franklin's arm. "Sure man, I'd like to ride in something beside Strum's old clunker for a change."

"You comin' Rufus?" Strum asked.

Naw, I got some action waitin' for me across town."

"We're goin' on then," said Franklin. "Ya'll catch up."

Out in the warm summer night, crickets seem to have their own band, serenading the gravel parking lot where Franklin's Pontiac GTO was parked behind the pub. Inside, the vehicle smelled of leather and chrome.

Mojo leaped into the back seat as Buddy settled up front in the passenger bucket seat.

Buddy ran his hand over the dash and along the center console and gear shift. "Pretty smooth for a piano man. What color is it?"

"Blue, naturally. We're musicians." Franklin laughed at his joke and tires spun against gravel as they sped from the parking lot.

As they traveled the elevated freeway, Buddy felt Franklin gear up to a speed Buddy knew had to be unsafe. But the car almost glided along the pavement with a smooth, quiet quality.

"It's a hella ride, Franklin."

"Yeah, she's one sweet baby."

"Just get us there in one piece."

Franklin slowed the car. "This our turn-off, West Sixth?"

"Yeah, take it down to Lafayette."

"Starting to sprinkle," Franklin said, slowing even more, guiding the car along the off ramp. "I'm not sure where the wiper switch is."

A loud screech of tires was followed by a curse from Franklin. "The son-of-a-bitch is forcing me off the road!"

The car slid sideways and Buddy fell forward, putting his hands out to catch the dashboard as the car slammed to a stop. "What the hell?"

Buddy's door was yanked open and he was pulled from the seat. The car rocked as the door was slammed behind, capturing Mojo inside as the dog came across the seat snarling. Buddy was being dragged across the pavement by two men while Mojo barked and starched at the car window. Buddy broke away long enough to pull the knife from his pocket and flip the blade open. He lunged at the man nearest him and felt the shaft bury into flesh.

"Damn!" a man yelled. "Bastard cut me!"

A blow to his face sent Buddy reeling back and the knife was knocked from his grasp. Two men grabbed him from behind.

"Whata you guys want?" Franklin was shouting. "Put that gun down. Let him go, he's blind."

"Shut that one up," a man said. "Don't kill him."

Buddy heard a thud as Franklin dropped to the ground.

A fist landed a blow to Buddy's stomach and he bent double with pain.

"Give us our stash or you've played your swan song blues boy."

"I don't have it," Buddy gasped. "Gave it to the cops."

A second blow to the stomach buckled Buddy's knees.

"You lying sack of shit. Where is it?" the voice demanded.

"Baton Rouge PD." Buddy was kneeling now, holding his abdomen; the soft rain catching in his hair and running down his face. "Tell 'em I sent you."

A boot caught him in the side and Buddy went face down on the wet pavement. Fifteen years ago he had fallen to the ground like this, unable to get up, losing consciousness for an almost deadly blow to his head. That blow had taken his sight. Back then it was gangs of teen-age boys wearing the colors of the Lords and the Vipers, challenging each other for no good reason except ownership of a dirty neighborhood street. Back then he had played the devil's game, always sure he could win. He knew better now. The stakes were higher.

"Shoot the bastard, man," a voice cried. "He cut me bad."

"No, we ain't 'spose to kill him."

"Let's break his hands so he cain't play the guitar no more," another voice said. "I seen that in a movie where they broke a pool shark's hands 'cause he cheated them."

Buddy pulled his hands beneath him, holding them between his chest and the cement, trying to protect them. He could hear Mojo barking inside the car and the rain growing stronger, pelting the ground. For the first time in his adult life, Buddy was truly afraid. If they broke his hands, they would take everything from him.

The glare of headlights raked across Buddy. From where he lay on the ground, Buddy could hear a car screech to a stop.

"What the hell's going on?"

Buddy wept with relief at the sound of Amos's voice.

"Let's go," the assailant said.

Buddy lay motionless as men shouted, footsteps ran across pavement, doors banged shut and a car careened away. He kept his hands folded against him even as arms lifted him up and held him because his legs had turned to water.

**

"How ya doing?" John Allen asked.

"Still sore," Buddy said. "I made some coffee."

"I'll get a cup." Allen scraped back a chair and sat across the kitchen table from him. "I thought you'd like to know we brought those four guys in. Picked 'em up last night."

"That was fast work." Buddy drank the strong coffee from his cup.

"It helped that Strum got the car's license number." Allen stood up. "I'll get that coffee."

Buddy waited while the detective walked to the counter, lifted a mug from the rack and poured hot coffee from the pot. When he sat back down, Allen said, "Franklin fingered them in a line-up. We charged them with assault and attempted carjacking."

"They weren't after the car."

"Said they were." Allen raked the sugar bowl across the table. "Said they wanted that classic GTO so they could piece it out on the market."

"That it?"

"Afraid so." Allen's spoon clanked against the cup. "They copped to that. Wouldn't budge on the drugs and we can't make 'em for it."

"It's the cocaine they were after. They said so."

"Anyway, they're off the street for now, Allen said. "The PD's got a guy from the narcotics unit following up."

Buddy wrapped his hands around his warm coffee mug, the heat felt reassuring on his fingers. "They were going to break my hands, John."

"Worst thing you can do to a musician, I guess, except kill 'em."

"Same thing," Buddy said.

He heard Allen take a slurp of the hot coffee and sit the cup down on the table.

"Be careful, Buddy," the cop said. "They're not the only ones and whoever sent them will try again."

Chapter Twenty-Six

"I don't think I've ever been inside your place before," Franklin said. "Just to the door and all. It's really nice."

Mojo moved past Buddy to greet the musician standing in the doorway. The dog whined a little, wanting to be petted.

"Hey, Mojo," Franklin said. "How ya'll doing, boy?"

"Come on in and sit down," Buddy said. "You want a Dr. Pepper or something?"

"Yeah, that'd be good."

"You don't mind helping yourself, they're in the fridge. Takes me too long to get over there and all."

"I'll get it, no problem," said Franklin.

Buddy sat on the arm of the sofa and waited for Franklin to walk across the room and into the kitchen. He heard the refrigerator door open and close and a noise as Franklin popped the top of a soda can.

"Can I bring you one?" Franklin asked.

"Not right now."

"Nice place ya'll got here," Franklin. "Ivy got it fixed up real pretty."

"So I'm told."

"Nice little piano. I like an upright. That's what I learned on."

"Me too," Buddy said. "A big, old, out of tune thing in my daddy's bar."

"Not sure I ever really heard you play the piano, just a few riffs here and there."

"Gave it up for the guitar."

Buddy heard Franklin raise the lid over the piano keys and run his hand across them. "Looks like you keep this one in good shape."

"I try. Ivy likes me to play so I accompany her sometime."

"She sure can sing."

"She likes jazz, but right now she's doing the blues for us. Took me a whole lot of convincing to make her believe you don't have to be sad to sing the blues."

The two men fell silent and the only sound was music drifting in from the bedroom radio. Buddy ran his finger down the scar on his face and decided it was time to bring up the reason Franklin was here in the middle of the afternoon.

"What'd the guy at the body shop say about the car damage?"

"Not too bad." Franklin seemed hesitant. "Mostly just scratch marks from Mojo trying to get out of the car."

"You took it to Thurman's over on Fifth Street, right?"

"Yeah. I thought he would do us right."

"They give you a price on the repairs?"

"Yeah, they did. It's pretty large." Franklin said. "I can use my insurance but my deductible is about a thousand dollars."

"Told you I'd take care of it. I'll go back down with you and have them put it on my credit card. Just let me get some shoes on."

Buddy stood up but Franklin stopped him, putting a hand on his arm.

"What was that all about, Buddy? They didn't want the car or they would have taken it right off."

"Told the police they wanted the car."

"I heard those guys, Buddy. They asked you for their stuff. What do you have of theirs that almost got us killed?"

This was a different Franklin that Buddy was hearing. There was determination in his voice. He was demanding to know the whole story. Well, thought Buddy, maybe he had a right.

"Cocaine," Buddy said. "A lot of cocaine."

Franklin sighed. "You using again or selling? Or both?"

"It's not like that, kid," Buddy said. "They were planting the stuff in my motor home. I didn't know it but I was their mule. What better than an unsuspecting blind guy to haul their merchandise; especially when we're on tour. It was pretty smart; that is until I found it."

"Then what?"

"I took it to the cops. They had it then and they still have it."

They were quiet now, the impact of the situation weighing in the air. Stan Getz' saxophone music came from the bedroom. Buddy knew Franklin wanted to trust him, but like everybody else, Franklin must be finding it hard to believe the story he was hearing. Buddy thought he had given them all the right not to believe him considering the years he had spent using.

"I cain't tell my dad about this," Franklin said. "He'll just freak out. Make me quit the band."

Buddy thought about that; Franklin's dad telling him he had to quit the band and him doing it. But down here, in the deep south, that's the way it often was. His dad would say he didn't want his boy getting into something where people were using drugs. It seemed to Buddy that Franklin's dad didn't know much about the music world his son worked in. Or about Franklin either for that matter.

"Look," Buddy said, "I don't know who put the dope there but it had to be someone who knows me."

"Not one of the band, I'm sure of that," declared Franklin in that innocent way of his that always seemed to drive Strum crazy.

"Are you? I'm not."

"Who?" asked an astonished Franklin.

"I don't know," Buddy said, almost to himself.

"Naw," Franklin said, "Naw. Cain't be anyone we know."

"I'd like it if you kept this between us," Buddy said. "I'm telling you because of your car and all, but the rest of the band don't know. Let's keep it that way."

"If that's what you want, Buddy. I won't say anything but I don't believe anyone we know would do it."

"Could be a lot of people," said Buddy. "Maybe the same one that killed Jake Washington and Nina. Stuck an ice pick in their ear."

"Holly shit!" Franklin exclaimed. "What are we in here? Hangin' with you can be dangerous. They don't get their dope back, we might get the ice pick treatment next."

They laughed, but Buddy knew it was no joke.

"No offense, but do you think we could leave Mojo here while we go on down to the body shop? I mean, you know, just getting the car fixed and all."

"Hear that Mojo? Franklin don't want you in his car. Don't get your feelings hurt now," Buddy teased. "Yeah, he'd be okay by himself long as we're not gone all day."

The ride to the body shop seemed a little uncomfortable to Buddy. Franklin asking when Ivy was coming back and Buddy telling him he wasn't sure, but she had wrapped up a couple of gigs for them in New York.

He didn't mention Carnegie Hall. He wanted her to tell the entire band when they were all together and see their reaction at the news.

Thurman greeted them warmly, pumping their hands and slapping their backs. He wore slacks and a shirt now, leaving the dirty work to his two sons and other employees in the shop. Thurman was a trombone player who sat in on an occasional job, but mostly he had joined the eight to five working world.

"Been hearing your new CD, Buddy on the radio. That good stuff," he said.

"It's doing pretty well," Buddy said. "Franklin'll bring you over a copy."

"Too bad about the GTO, but I think we can put it back like new," Thurman said. "Mojo must have been pretty mad."

Buddy handed him a credit card. "Put the deducible on this."

"Sure thing." Thurman took the card.

Franklin put a pen in Buddy's hand and placed it on a paper. "Sign here."

"Be good as new in a couple of days," Thurman said. "I'll give you a call Franklin."

Buddy stuck out his hand, "Good to see you, man."

On the ride home, Buddy wondered mildly what Ivy would say about the large charge on the Visa card. He'd have to tell her just what he had told the police; that someone had tried to carjack the GTO.

Franklin walked with him to the door of the condo. They could hear Mojo whining on the other side.

"Remember," Buddy said as he unlocked the door, "that conversation we had earlier? We need to keep that between the two of us."

Chapter Twenty-Seven

"Buddy? This is Tom Jordan," the voice on the phone said. "You know, from your daddy's bar?"

"Tom?" Buddy held the phone, trying to figure out why this man was calling him. "What's happening? Anything wrong?

"No. Everything's okay. I just thought you should know I brought Jimmy home from the hospital this morning. He told me not to call you but I'm calling anyway. Thought you should know."

Buddy was silent, thinking of Jimmy calling one of the bar regulars to take him home from the hospital. He imagined the hospital clerk asking Jimmy if they should call his son and him saying, "No, we won't bother him. He's blind, you know and can't drive. Just call my friend, Tom, he'll come for me."

But Buddy knew it was more than that. He knew Jimmy didn't want to see him, was blaming him for the beating he took because he believed Buddy was still involved in drugs.

"Are you there, son?" Tom Jordan asked.

"I'm here."

"Just thought you should know," Jordan said, like he didn't know what else to say. "Maybe he needs someone with him. He's there alone."

"I'll go over."

"You need me, I'll come get you."

"Thanks, I'll get a cab."

"Got your number off the wall by the bar phone," Tom went on. "Calling from my house though. Thought I should let you know."

"I'm obliged to you, Tom," Buddy was anxious to hang up. "I'll be on my way."

He called a taxi and told the driver to take him to Spanish Town, to Jimmy O'Brian's Irish Pub, did he know the place?

"Sure, I know it," the driver answered. "You goin' there alone? I mean being blind and all?"

"I'll be fine. I grew up there."

The door to the bar was locked when Buddy got there. He pushed on the door, but it held securely in place. He pounded against it and called out but no one came. Mojo barked in protest until Buddy hushed him.

"Place is closed," the cab driver said, standing beside him. "Want me to carry you somewhere else?"

"No. This' my old man's place. I'll get in."

"You got a key?"

"Yeah, I got a key." Buddy pulled a ring of keys from his pocket. "Wanta help me find the right one? I think it's an old one, almost worn out. "

The driver smelled of sweat and tobacco. He took the keys and said, "This here's a Yale and so is the lock. Must be it."

Buddy heard the rattle as the lock opened. He thought that the lock had rattled as long back as he could remember. Mojo moved, restless beside him, wanting to go inside.

"There ya go," the driver said, putting the keys into Buddy's hand. "Dark in there. Want me to go in with you?"

"It's always dark wherever I go," Buddy said, placing a twenty dollar bill with a corner fold in the man's hand. "I'll be fine, got my dog. Thanks."

"You already paid me," the driver protested.

"Keep it," Buddy said. "Thanks for the extra help."

"My name is Warren. You call the company for a ride back, ask for me."

"I'll do that."

Buddy pushed the diamond tuff padded door open and went in. The eerie quiet surrounded him, and he reached down to touch Mojo. There was none of the ching of the old cash register, no rumble of voices, and no music from the jukebox. Not even the swing bands that Jimmy listened to when he was alone. Buddy heard his own footsteps and the click of Mojo's nails as they walked across the floor.

"Jimmy?" he called.

No answer. The silence moved in on Buddy like rising water.

Holding onto Mojo's harness and moving his cane back and forth in front of him, Buddy made his way to the old upright piano. He sat down on the bench and raised the lid from the keys. Mojo settled on the floor and Buddy began to play *Memories of You*. He played soft and low on the old, out of tune piano, every note coming from his mind, rifting in the middle of the song, giving it tenderness. He began to sing quietly:

Waking skies at sunrise, every sunset too—

Mojo sat up and a board creaked as a footstep tread across the room. A second voice finished the song; *And they all, just recall memories of you.*

Buddy finished the song and laid his hands flat against the keys. No one spoke until Jimmy said, "How'd ya know I was here?"

"Tom Jordan called. You should have called, Jimmy."

"My heart is broken. I love you too much, me boy. Sure and you're all I have left in this world."

"Then believe me Jimmy. Let's get this straight between us. I came to tell you again that the drugs are not mine and I am not using or selling. Someone, I don't know who, put them in the motor home for transporting. I'm sorry they hurt you."

"Ivy?"

"She's still in New York," Buddy said. "I want her to stay there until this is all worked out."

"What does she know?"

"Nothing. I don't want her to be involved."

"Tis a fine mess, then."

"The police have the drugs, Jimmy. I gave them to John Allen, a cop friend of mine."

"That will be the end of it then," Jimmy said with relief. "Can you play some more Benny Goodman now while I serve up some Irish stew for you and me and maybe a dish for Mojo?"

As Buddy played the opening phrase of *Don't Be That Way*, he heard Jimmy walk across the room toward the living quarters. Let Jimmy believe what he wanted, but Buddy knew that turning the drugs over to the police was not the end of anything.

Chapter Twenty-Eight

Buddy and Amos entered the rehearsal hall to the random ring of cymbals and drum taps, piano keys running scales, voices engaged in various conversations and bursts of laughter. Beside Buddy, Mojo stopped as someone approached. Buddy felt Amos touch his hand as a signal to hold up.

An oil slick voice said, "Buddy, its Art Kimble here. They told me you'd be rehearsing this morning so I came down."

"Whatdaya want, Art?" Buddy didn't hide the hostility he harbored for the radio station owner.

"There's something I think you should know. It's about your CD."

"You talk to Ivy?"

"I heard she's out of town. I think I should tell you."

Buddy dropped his hand from Amos' arm. "Go on Amos. I'll be there in a minute."

Amos walked away and Buddy shifted the weight of the soft guitar case on his shoulder to an easier position. The dark shadow of Art Kimble stood before him, a tall, slender man. It was if he was waiting for a signal to speak.

"What is it?" Buddy asked.

"Just thought you should know," Art said in that smooth, salesman voice. "Your old manager, Eldon, has been trying to get your new CD blackballed. Called the station and tried to persuade us not to play it. Probably calling all the other stations too. He says you owe him rights."

"Are they to listening to him?"

"Not me. But I can't talk for the others."

Buddy ran his fingers over the scar on his face and tugged at the loop in his ear. "Why you holding out?"

"I know you and I are not friends, but I don't want this to hurt Ivy's chances of something big."

There it was, something Buddy had known all along. Art had the hots for Ivy and now he was making no bones about it. It was all about Ivy with this guy, not Buddy, the band, the music or honesty.

"I'll deal with Eldon," Buddy said.

"You'll tell Ivy I came to you on this?"

"Yeah, I'll tell her." Buddy tugged at Mojo's harness and started to walk away. He stopped and turned back. "I know you want Ivy and she's a free soul. But you're wasting your time, man."

"I've never pretended it was any other way," Art said, walking off, his voice more distant. "And I don't usually waste my time."

Art's footsteps sounded down the old wood floor. Buddy wanted to follow him and kick his ass. But he had enough to deal with, what with Jimmy hurt, and drug dealers using the RV to move their cocaine. They'd be coming for him soon, he was sure of that.

He settled on a stool and pulled the guitar from its case. Putting the strap over his head and shoulder, he ran his fingers down the familiar strings, drawing strength from the feel of them. He picked out the first notes of his theme song, and he was home again. Nothing else mattered except the music.

"Heard Jimmy had some trouble," Rufus said.

Buddy turned toward the voice behind his left shoulder. Stale whiskey breath met him.

"He's a tough old hide," Buddy said.

"The word is he was beat up pretty bad."

"He'll recover." Buddy turned back to the guitar, rifting the tune in his head and on the strings. "Just some low life scum trying to rob the bar."

"Maybe," Rufus said. "Maybe not."

Buddy laid his hand flat against the guitar face to silence the sound. "You know something I don't?"

"Naw. Just thinking what could happen next. Might be they was looking for you."

"Why would they come after me?"

The air was tense between them, words laying there unsaid. Buddy was holding on, keeping in check. Everything was coming at him and he had to hold back, wait until the time was right.

"Let's get started," Strum yelled. "I gotta get home sometime tonight."

**

Back in the condo with the fragrance of Ivy all around him, Buddy was missing her more than ever. He needed her to call tonight, for her to reassure him as she always did, and he would tell her about Eldon, the two them talking it over. He listened to jazz coming from the other room and remembered her laugh, her hand squeezing his. The old urge for Jack Daniels grew strong, making him weak, making him tremble inside and his skin crawl as if a spider moved up his back. He picked up the phone and called Carolyn.

"Detective Hunter."

"Hey, doll."

"Hey, Buddy." Her voice softened.

"I'm thinking of crab legs for dinner. You in?"

"Where?"

"Louie's House of Blues in Spanish Town."

"I'll pick you up in an hour." There was eagerness in her voice. It caused his imagination to wander past dinner to the smell of soap and a darkened bedroom.

He fed Mojo and called Jason to ask if he would take the dog for the night because he might not be back until morning.

"Sure, I'm not going anywhere, got an exam tomorrow so I'll be hitting the books tonight. I'll take him for a run before I bring him home."

When the dog was gone, Buddy took a shower and shaved. He dressed in fresh jeans, a polo shirt, and loafers. He refused to listen to the voice in his head that told him a shot of Jack would take it all away, black out the troubles moving in on him. A knock on the door brought him back, away from the dark liquid that beckoned.

"Carolyn?"

"It's me," she said. "Your ride waits."

He opened the door, touched her face and her hair with his fingertips. "You look like a million bucks."

"Well, maybe half a million," she said and laughed.

It would be all right for a few hours. He could hold out with Carolyn beside him, making him laugh, forgetting the Eldons, Arts, and Rufus' of the world. He could push Jack Daniels to the back of his mind and say no to the liquid allure one more time.

The blues band on stage at Louie's was old friends of Buddy's and they nodded a greeting when he came in. Half way through the first set the leader, Stan Cooper, stopped the music.

"We got a blues genius in the audience, ladies and gentlemen," Cooper said. "Buddy O'Brian. Let's get Blind Buddy on up for a number."

Buddy waved and shook his head, but the applause rose, insisting he play. He was tired and moody, and didn't have a guitar with him. The applause continued until Cooper stepped off the stage and come to escort Buddy to the front.

"Go ahead, Buddy," Carolyn urged.

Seeing no polite way out of it, he stood up and walked across the room with Cooper. Up on the stage, Buddy took the guitar handed to him, leaned into the microphone and said, "I wrote this song and it's on my new CD with the same name. It's *Last Call* and it's for you, Carolyn."

He sang *Last Call* in a slow, front porch style, his voice gravel and water, heavy with emotion. It was a song he had written from somewhere deep in his gut and he made love to it, meaning every word, every note when he sang. The crowd seemed to believe him as he sang, thundering applause as he finished, handed the guitar away, and took a bow.

When he returned to the table Carolyn kissed him lightly, whispering "thank you."

"You starting to like the blues now?" he teased.

"I like the blues maker."

"That's cool," he reached across the table to take her hand, "because he likes you."

A coarse laugh came from someone standing at the table. "Well, ain't this cozy. Does Ivy know about this little tryst?"

Carolyn pulled her hand away.

"Get lost Eldon," Buddy said without raising his head.

"Not a chance lover boy. Been looking in every joint in town for you."

Buddy stood up. He could feel the heat and smell the alcoholic sweat of Eldon's body. "You found me."

"I want my cut of the CD sales or I'm gona blackball you with every disk jockey in the country." Eldon slurred his words, his tall, skinny shadow swaying as he pushed a finger in Buddy's chest.

Buddy slid his hand in his pocket, his fingers curling around the switchblade. "Poke me with that finger again and I'll cut it off."

Carolyn was on her feet. "Baton Rouge Police. Move on Eldon or find yourself in the city slam. The folks here don't want trouble."

"You jokin' now honey. Pretty girl like you carrying that badge." Eldon laughed a drunken laugh. "I'll catch up with this blind boy later when he don't have a woman to protect him."

It wasn't until he heard glass breaking and a woman scream that Buddy realized he had cut Eldon and knocked him across a table and to the floor. Arms were holding him and Stan Cooper was saying "Let it go, man."

"Here, wrap this around your arm," he heard someone say.

"Leave me alone," Eldon growled.

Carolyn was speaking to the waiter, paying the bill, cajoling the club owner, and then she said, "Let's go Buddy."

The summer night was soft as silk on the street where the traffic noise rushed around them. Buddy gripped knife in his pocket, damp with Eldon's blood, and waited for the throbbing in his temples to stop and the heat in his face to cool. They walked down the block, neither of them speaking.

When they reached her car, Carolyn stopped and put her arms around Buddy pressing her hard, runner's body against him. Her kiss made promises, and right now, he needed her to keep them. He put his hand behind her head and pulled her mouth into his, feeling her lips part and her tongue touch his. When he let her go, her breath was warm on his cheek.

"We can go to my place," she said.

Chapter Twenty-Nine

As they made love, Buddy willed each caress to press open the secret door and move him into the escape he needed, into that place of peace where pain did not exist. Jack Daniels could always take him there. But even as Carolyn cried out in pleasure, he knew he was just hanging on to sanity.

Tonight she was his substitute for Jack Daniels. But it wasn't working out. He felt empty. The whiskey had never let him down.

As aggressive as she was in bed and as quickly as she reacted to his every move, when it was over, Carolyn did not cling to him. Ivy always wrapped herself around him, holding him in sleep as if he might vanish in the night. But Carolyn moved to her own space near the edge of the bed, curling up alone, satisfied, and breaking the connection.

He lay awake, wondering if she kept any alcohol in the apartment, fighting the urge to get out of bed and search in unknown cabinets. He thought of leaving, of searching for a taxi in the dim light and empty streets of early morning.

In this silent, unfamiliar room, he knew Ivy must have called home last night, and that Mojo was restless without him.

He remembered the day he found Mojo. He and Ivy were walking in the neighborhood park, and the sun had the bright warmth of late spring. A breeze kept the heat away and the smell of freshly mowed grass and blooming flowers waffled through the air. An impromptu band played for coins tossed into an open guitar case and they stopped to listen.

"Sit here on this bench and I'll go get us something to drink," Ivy said. "I won't be long."

He was almost nineteen then, just out of the Missouri School for the Blind. As angry as he had been three years before when he and Jimmy made the trip to the school, he had been just as afraid to leave it. There had been safety there and friendships among the other sightless students and a special connection with those who played in the band. There had been packages of food sent from families back in their home towns, shared in late night talks in dorm rooms. There was the day Buddy had backed Rhonda against the music room wall and kissed her.

"I like you a lot, Rhonda."

"I feel the same about you, Buddy. It's fine while we are here in this school, but we're two blind kids. Out in the world, we need sighted people."

They went their own separate ways after graduation and the vow to stay in touch was already broken.

Back in Baton Rouge, he struggled with uncertainties like a man in the water, swimming toward a shore that he cannot see, unsure that it is even there. Jimmy and Ivy, in their constant hovering, made him want to throw them off with a scream.

Now, in the park, he was glad to be alone for a while. The quartet was playing *Do You Know What it Means to Miss New Orleans?* Their loose Dixieland style included a slide trombone, a trumpet, a snare drum, and a guitar. The drum fell behind in the beat and the trumpet slid off its note. The guitar man was mediocre and Buddy's fingers moved against his leg, trying to correct each missed chord.

Something small and warm wiggled against Buddy's leg. He reached one hand down and touched the head of a puppy, which immediately washed his fingers with its tongue. Buddy picked him up. Couldn't be more than a couple of months old, he thought. It was a good feeling holding the writhing dog whose mouth found Buddy's face.

"Who you got there?" Ivy said with a little laugh in her voice.

"I don't know, he just came up to me."

"Cute little guy. Looks like a German Shepard."

"What color?"

"Black with brown markings."

"His owner around?"

"Don't see anyone. Here's your soda."

Ivy put the cup in Buddy's hand and he reached in for some pieces of ice. He held them in his open palm for the puppy that licked at them thirstily.

"Get him a hotdog, will you, Ivy? I think he's hungry."

"Oh, Buddy." Ivy sighed and stood up. "Okay, I'll be right back."

The dog settled into Buddy's arms while he stroked the animal and sang in a quiet way as the band played *Bill Bailey.*

A voice standing just above him said, "You Buddy O'Brian? Used to belong to the Lords over on Sixth Street?"

"Who's asking?" Buddy reached for the thin white cane lying beside him, that old wariness coming back.

"Jerry Casey. I was a Lord too. This' my band playing here."

"How ya doin', Jerry?"

"Heard they put out your eyes in that last rumble. Sorry about that."

"You playin' the slide?" Buddy wanted to change the subject. He didn't want to talk about the old days.

"That's me. You used to play piano, didn't you?"

"Mostly guitar now."

"You wanta sit in? We can do something besides Dixieland; it's just that people seem to like it out here."

The dog wiggled against Buddy's chest and he put it on the ground. "Yeah, I'll sit in if I can borrow a guitar. You guys know any Fats Domino?"

One of the musicians handed over his instrument and Buddy stood with the rest of the group, playing the old rhythm and blues songs. The puppy curled up at his feet and lay there in spite of Buddy's toe tapping. When he gave the owner back his guitar, Buddy stayed put and sang with the group. A small crowd gathered to listen and applaud. For an afternoon in the breezy sun, Buddy didn't care about all the things that had troubled him just a few hours ago. His anger left and he was free. It was a feeling that came with each note. This was where he lived, where his soul was.

"Sun's going down; people going home to supper. We'll pack in for today," Casey said. "You're welcome to a share of the tip money."

"No thanks. It was a gas just sittin' in."

Hand shakes all around, slaps on the shoulder, and "come back next week." Then Ivy was there, taking his arm, walking him away. The dog bounced along beside his leg.

"That dog is following you," Ivy said.

Buddy reached down and picked him up. "Think I'll call him Mojo."

**

Carolyn poured Buddy a cup of coffee, leaning over him so that he felt the terry cloth of her bath robe and the moisture on her skin. She kissed his cheek, and her hair, still wet from the shower they had taken together, brushed across his face.

"It's been good," she said.

"Uh-huh." He was no longer interested. The demons were gone and his mind had traveled on. He wanted to get back to the condo to check if Ivy left a message, and to see about Mojo.

"I'm a little worried about my dog. Jason, the kid takin' care of him, might need to go somewhere. Could you carry me home?"

"Sure." She drew back at the dismissal in his voice. "I have to go to work anyway."

They were quiet in the car. There didn't seem to be anything to say after all that passion last night that seemed to have burned out like a candle that had held a flame too long. Carolyn reached for his hand, but he sat passive, not curling his fingers around hers as he would have before.

The summer day was hot and sultry, the temperature climbing. When they got out of the car, the humidity slapped Buddy in the face like a hot wash cloth. They walked to the condo and as he pushed the key into the lock, the door swung open before he could turn it.

Ivy?" he called.

Carolyn put her hand on his arm. "Hold it."

He was close enough to feel her reaching for the nine millimeter in a holster at her waist. She moved him aside and stepped into the condo. "Good God!"

"What?"

"Someone tossed this place."

"What the hell!"

"Stay here for a minute while I check it out."

He heard the jazz floating in from the bedroom, but the condo felt different, a blur of cloudy images spread across the room. Carolyn came back, relief in her voice as she called police dispatch.

"My guitars still in the bedroom?" Buddy asked as she flipped her cell phone shut.

"I saw three over by the closet, pulled out of the cases but they looked okay. Police will be here in a minute to dust the place and make a report."

"Can't let Ivy come home to this," Buddy said.

"I'll call my housekeeper and see if she can come over and straighten it up."

Buddy sat down on a dining room chair and fingered the scar on his face. "They were looking for the cocaine."

"I think so."

"Jimmy in the hospital and now this."

Carolyn put her hand on his shoulder. "It's not your fault."

Maybe not, he thought, but it happened because of me. The anger boiling up inside him was like fire under his skin. Hold on, a voice inside him whispered, hold on.

"Detective Hunter?" A male voice came in the door with several shadows.

"Hello Sam," Carolyn greeted them. "This is Buddy O'Brian, he lives here."

"You that blues singer? Wow, they did a number on the place, didn't they?"

Buddy said nothing. Hold on, the voice inside repeated.

"We'll get some prints and get out of here," the voice said. "You just come home and find it this way?"

"I'll write the report," Carolyn said. "There's a cleaning lady coming over in a while to put things back."

Buddy sat in a stupor, his feelings of violation and anger boiling inside. He was only half listening to men talking to each other, laughing, moving about his home. The light banner as they worked seemed to be all about their kid's soccer game or some hamburger place they found uptown, or the waitress at the coffee shop. Remarkable, Buddy mused, how fast they were, how quickly they were gone. Carolyn stayed until they left and then followed them out the door, promising to come back after her watch. The relief he felt when the door closed behind the last of them was like a splinter pulled from beneath a fingernail.

The door opened again and he heard a low whistle. "Damn, what happened here?" Jason said.

Mojo ran to Buddy, nuzzling him with his nose, whining. Buddy took the dog's ears in his hands and held him close to his face, the dog licking his cheeks. "I'm okay, boy, I'm okay."

"I gotta get to class for the exam," Jason said. "You gonna be alright?"

"Someone broke in last night," Buddy said. I got a woman coming to clean. Don't worry, Mojo's with me."

Everyone was gone. The silence rang around him, except for the music, low and mellow as it traveled in from the bedroom. He got up to make coffee because he didn't know what else to do, but the kitchen was too confusing, scattered with utensils, pots and pans. So, he sat down and waited until the doorbell rang and a woman called out, "Mr. O'Brian? I'm the cleaning lady Ms. Hunter asked to come over."

Elsie, she said her name was, and she chatted constantly as she moved from room to room, setting things upright, asking where they belonged, putting them back in place.

"My brother, Leroy, got his house broken into a couple months ago," she rattled on. "Didn't make this big a mess though. They said kids did it. I swear Baton Rouge getting' to be a bad place to live."

Buddy paid no attention to what she said, wishing she would finish up and leave. He was so tired, as if he'd walked a thousand miles to get to this weary moment.

"Don't know where you'd move to though," she went on, "ever place else jes as bad."

The doorbell rang and Elsie called out, "I'll get it."

"James O'Brian here?" A man's voice said. It was the voice of authority. Buddy had heard it often enough to know.

"Here," Buddy said.

"Mr. O'Brian, I'm Sergeant Miller, Baton Rouge Police. I have to ask you to come down to the station with me."

"Because of this break in?"

"No sir. I'm investigating a murder."

Chapter Thirty

"He have to have that dog in here with him?"

"He's blind."

"Yeah? Well he can't take him into the interrogation room."

It amused Buddy that the two detectives were talking about him as if he were not there. He wanted to tell them that he was blind but his hearing was fine.

The whirl of overhead fans droned on while phones rang incessantly. Decades of Louisiana rain and heat captured in the rock walls and worn wood floors of the old Baton Rouge police station exuded a moldy smell that no amount of cleaning or paint could eradicate.

"Can your dog stay out here, Mr. O'Brian?"

Buddy patted Mojo. "Lay down, boy. Stay here."

Detective Miller took Buddy's arm and led him into a room. "Come in here and have a seat."

Buddy felt the metal of a hardback chair and lowered himself into it. He reached out and touched a table in front of him. "What's this about?"

"You know an Elton Dubois?"

"Used to be my manager. Fired him a few months ago."

"Word is that you had a run-in with him last night over at Louie's. Heard you cut him up some." Miller's voice took a hard edge.

"Who told you that?"

"Got an anonymous phone call this morning."

"Elton came up to the table while I was having dinner and started trouble." Buddy ran the flat of his hand across the scar on his cheek. "He file an assault charge?"

"Could be he planned to do that." Miller had been standing but the rake of a chair indicated that he sat down. Buddy felt Miller lean across the table, the smell of cheap aftershave coming toward him. "But someone stopped him before he got a chance."

"How's that?" Buddy said.

"They cut his throat."

The room felt like a ship rocking on high seas, turning in the wind and titling on angry waves. Buddy grabbed the table with both hands to steady his mind. The crash of glass as Eldon fell over a table rang in Buddy's head.

"You thinkin' I did it?"

"You had reason to," Miller moved back across the table. "He was giving you grief over your new CD. He was calling the stations and telling them not to play it."

"Yeah, but I didn't off him."

"I understand you're pretty quick with a knife."

Buddy tried to relax, move the tension from his body. "Blind musician plays in blues dives needs some protection."

"You carrying now?'

"No."

"Where's your blade?'

"Left it at the house. Got more sense than to bring it to the cop farm."

"We need to look at it." Miller got up and walked around the room, the rubber soles of his shoes squeaking on the cement floor. "Where'd you go when you left the restaurant?"

A rap on the door brought Miller to a stop. Someone entered the room and said, "I'm John Allen, Selby County Sheriff's Department. I'd like to sit in on this. Saw the report on the state-wide bulletins this morning. It may connect to a murder in Memphis."

Buddy half rose from the chair and put out his hand. "How's it goin' John?"

Allen walked across the room and shook Buddy's hand. "I feel like this has something to do with the murders of Jake Washington and Nina Boxer. I want to check that out."

"Your friend here is on top of the list of suspects," Miller said from behind Allen. "Seems the woman he lives with is out of town and his father was in the hospital as the result of a mugging. Last night, Mr. O'Brian assaulted Elton Dubois, and Dubois was found dead this morning."

"I don't think Buddy's our man on this one," Allen said. "Can you tell us where you were last night and who you were with, Buddy?"

It was so ironic that Buddy almost smiled. Clearly he wasn't home while his house was being tossed. He had gone off on Eldon last night in a public place. Could he tell Allen that he was in bed with his woman all night? Would she back him up if he did?

"Am I being charged with something here?" Buddy said.

"No, just give us an alibi and you're out of here. Where'd you go when you left Louie's?"

Buddy reached up and touched the gold loop in his ear. No matter how he answered a trap door would open underneath him and he would fall into a pit.

"I think I'll call an attorney, fellas. Can someone take me on home now?"

There was silence in the room. Buddy could hear the irritation in the detective's voice when he finally spoke. "Yeah. We'll take you home. We'll follow with a search warrant for that knife."

"No need for that, I'll give it to you." Buddy rose from the chair. "I'd like to get my dog and go now."

"You need to just work with us Buddy," Allen said. "We can clear this up."

There were three shadows in the room now, one standing just inside the door. As he walked past, he could smell the fresh scent of Carolyn. He knew it well now, and his memory flashed on whispered words of passion and fingers clutching his back. He hesitated, and then went through to the squad room. Her silence told him she would not help him, not with her boyfriend, John Allen and her fellow detectives standing there. She had too much to lose. He was completely alone. It was a feeling he was old friends with.

Detective Miller and Buddy did not speak on the way home. Miller came into the condo with Buddy and Mojo. He waited by the door while Buddy lifted the lid from the piano keys and retrieved his knife from its hiding place. Miller opened a plastic bag and Buddy dropped the mother-of-pearl handled switchblade into it.

"This it?" Miller asked.

"Only one I got."

"You know it's illegal to own one of these," Miller looked at the weapon, turning the clear bag in his hand.

"Lots of things against the law. People do them anyway."

"Sign this paper. It's a receipt that I took your property."

Miller put a pen in Buddy's hand and guided it a spot, bracing it on the hard surface of the piano.

"You got a shaky past O'Brian and if you murdered this guy, we'll put you away for it. I'm on my way to Louie's Crab Place to find out just what went down last night between you and Dubois."

"I'm a musician, not a killer."

"Come up with an alibi or you'll be singing the blues in the jailhouse." Miller walked away, leaving the door open.

Buddy closed the door and flipped the lock. He went into the kitchen and ran his hands over the counter top until he came to the coffee maker. Everything appeared to be back in place thanks to Elsie who seemed to be able to work as fast as she could talk. Finding the grounds and filter, he poured water into the top of the tank, holding his fingers inside to measure the right amount. A rich aroma filled the room along with the drip of coffee into the carafe. But what he really wanted—needed—was a bottle of Jack Daniels. His hands shook at the thought of it and he ran his fingers through his hair trying to steady himself.

He could call the drugstore, have them send over a fifth. He picked up the phone and held it for a minute before he dialed Strum's number.

"Hello?" A soft voice answered.

"How you doing, sweetheart?" Buddy said to Strum's wife, Ruthie. "I need to talk to Strum."

"Sompin' wrong?"

"No. Just want to talk to him."

"He ain't here right now, Buddy. I'll let him know you're looking for him. Ivy back from New York?"

"Not yet." Buddy was anxious to hang up. He began to walk the floor with the receiver to his ear. "Tell Strum I need him."

Buddy hung up, his skin was crawling and the desire for a drink was growing as the paced the kitchen floor. He touched the automatic dial for the small grocery-deli store on the corner where Ivy and he sent out for sandwiches and small food items. When the voice came on, he asked them to deliver a bottle of Jack Daniels Black Label.

Chapter Thirty-One

Strum was laughing and Buddy opened his eyes to the sound, coming up from the deep sleep he was in, lying face down on soft cushions. For a minute he didn't know where he was, the fog in his head was too thick to recognize the smells and sounds around him. There was faint music and Strum's voice.

"No way, man," he was saying, "you don't have three of a kind again. You a cheatin' dog."

"Where'd you learn to play poker? In the church basement?" It was Amos talking now, laughing with Strum.

Buddy raised his head, disoriented. It felt as if he had been whacked with a baseball bat. He was in his living room; he knew that now, on his sofa. Remembering the bottle of Jack Daniels, he felt around on the floor.

"You got my bottle?" he asked in a horse voice.

"Well lookie here. Back from the dead." Amos said. The shuffling of cards made a ruffling sound as they slapped against each other.

"We drank all your hooch," Strum added. "You left us almost half a bottle."

Buddy struggled to sit up. "What're you doing here, anyway?"

"Enjoying your hospitality," Amos said. "I don't get that expensive Black Label stuff very often. Not much in your fridge though."

Buddy leaned forward, his head in his hands. "Guess I fell asleep. Help me to the bathroom."

Strum took him by the elbow and they walked to the back, through the bedroom to the bath. Buddy turned on the cold water, caught it in his cupped hands and splashed it in his face and hair. Strum handed him a towel and Buddy buried his face in its cool dampness.

"Ruthie said you needed help," Strum said. "The front door was unlocked and I came on in. Saw that you started your party without me so I hung around."

"Do you know about Eldon?"

"Heard it on the news while ago."

"They think I did it."

"Did you?"

"Hell no. Why you ask me that, Strum?"

"Jes' gettin' it out the way."

Amos called from the living room, and it was like a rifle shot to Buddy head. "Want me to send for a pizza or ya'll want to go out for some ribs?"

"Can you make it if we go out?" Strum asked. "Better rinse that mouth, you smell like a whiskey factory."

"I'm shaky but I'll be okay." Buddy brushed his teeth and ran a comb through his thick curls. "How long you been here?'

"Four, maybe five hours. Called Amos to keep me company."

"Did Ivy call?"

"Yeah, she did. Told her you were asleep."

Buddy was pulling on a clean shirt. "Say anything else?"

"Wanted to know where you were last couple of times she called."

Buddy slipped on a pair of loafers. "I got a big problem, man."

"You been sleepin' in the wrong bed?"

"Yeah, but that ain't half of it. I was with Carolyn."

"You jivin' me? The woman cop?"

"That other cop's main squeeze?" Amos spoke from the doorway. He came over and put a cup of coffee in Buddy's hand. "For a blind dude, you sure like livin'on the edge."

"You gots an alibi man," Strum said. "What's better than the heat stickin' up for you?"

"You don't understand," Buddy said, taking a sip from the coffee cup. "she's not going to do that. I got to get my own way out of this."

"Kiss your ass good-bye," Amos sighed. "You done dipped in the wrong inkwell this time."

"Ivy finds out, you're double dead. Cops don't kill you, she will." Strum laughed.

"Let's go on down to Grandpa's Barbecue and get some ribs," Amos said. "We got to think up an alibi for Buddy. Say, that sounds like the name of a blues tune, don't it?"

Amos drove them to the edge of Spanish Town where Grandpa's Barbecue was located at the end of a block. The spicy aroma of meat grilling over live oak wood, and smoke drifting in the breeze drew them into the cement block building. Strum and Amos joked about the hand painted sign lit by a single light above it and the interior walls that had needed painting for as long as anyone could remember. Grandpa's shuffling steps came to their table. No one knew how old he was, but he smoked ribs all day and served them in the evening.

"What'll it be?" he asked in a raspy voice.

"Pork ribs, cold slaw, hot biscuits and butter," Amos ordered without consulting the others. No one disagreed. "Beer for us, hot coffee for him."

"Sweet ice tea," Buddy corrected.

A lone musician played an acoustic guitar, the sound almost drowned out by the noise of customer's conversation and laughter. He was doing a blues-folk song from the 1960s that grated on Buddy's raw nerves.

"The hell is he trying to do on that guitar?" he asked, drinking from the fruit jar of ice tea someone put in his hand. "The D string is out of tune."

"Never mind," Strum said. "Here's the ribs and slaw. Ribs at twelve o'clock, slaw at two."

"Mum-mum," Amos declared around a mouthful of food. "That's what I like about the south."

Buddy began to feel better as the sugar from the tea, the spice of the meat, and the tart creaminess of the cold slaw brought his blood pumping again. Even his head stopped its dull roar and was quiet.

"What they hiring a guy like that to play for?" he asked.

"Grandpa said the band didn't show, just this guy. "Doing the best he can, I guess."

"Voice is okay. Needs a lot of help with that instrument."

"You know," Amos said, placing his beer mug on the table with a thump, "I been knowing Grandpa a long time. Maybe I can help him out."

"It's an acoustic guitar," Buddy said. "No one will hear you."

"They got a piano. You want to come along? Sing for your supper?"

Buddy hesitated. Music was the only thing in the world that made him happy and took him to that other place where even Jack Daniels could not transport him. "Give me your arm."

Strum chuckled. "I'll just sit here and listen."

The guitar player on stage voiced astonishment as he recognized the two famous musicians walk up to the stage. "Hey," he said, "ain't you Blind Buddy?"

"Loan me your guitar, kid, and we'll jam a little," Amos said. "You want to sing with us?"

"Well, yeah, sure." He handed the cheap, beat-up guitar to Amos who spent a moment twisting the strings into tune. Buddy ran his hands over the ancient piano keyboard and found only a couple of the ivory tops missing. Amos began to sing a John Lee Hooker song, his mouth close to the microphone, tapping his foot as he played. Buddy followed the traditional blues style, playing the old upright as if he was in a jute joint in the early days of blues music. He ignored the sweat that wet his hair and trickled down his face as the alcohol he drank hours ago left his body.

They played without stopping for more than an hour, reaching back to the era of blues pioneers such as Blind Lemon and Hubbie Ledbetter, ending with *Midnight Special*. By this time, the crowd was clapping their hands and singing along. Amos handed the guitar back to the young musician and took Buddy's arm to lead him from the stage. People were still clapping as they made their way through the room where Strum sat.

Back at the table, Strum declared that was enough fun for the night. "I need to get on home to Ruthie before she finds another man."

"Be smart if she did," Buddy said.

They dropped Strum at his house and drove to the condo, the streets quiet in the summer night. Once inside, Amos said, "How about I make some coffee?"

"Go ahead, you want some."

"Okay with you, I'll crash here tonight."

Anger filled Buddy like a flash flood. He knew Amos was playing the role of caretaker, seeing that Buddy didn't order another bottle as soon as he was alone. Buddy gritted his teeth and said, "Extra bedroom. Help yourself."

"I'll just stretch out here on the sofa, maybe catch Jay Leno." Amos was in the kitchen, opening cabinet doors.

"I'm going on to bed," Buddy said.

"Buddy," Amos' voice was dead serious now, "I'll stand your alibi. I'll say you spent the night at my place last night."

Chapter Thirty-Two

When Buddy got up the next morning, Amos was gone. But he had brewed coffee before he left, and the rich aroma drifted from the kitchen. Buddy poured a mug just as Justin showed up to take Mojo for a run.

Left alone, Buddy leaned against the kitchen counter and took a sip from the steaming mug. He was feeling better about the whole Eldon situation now since Amos and he worked out a story saying they were together after he left Louie's.

The phone rang and he picked it up. "Yeah?"

"Buddy, where have you been?" Ivy said.

"Hey sweet baby. How's the Big Apple?"

"I think I have the whole thing wrapped up. Booked us into two clubs and as for Carnegie Hall, we'll sign the contract tomorrow. It was kind of tough getting what I wanted, but it looks good."

"That's my doll. Carnegie Hall. I'm proud of you. When's it set for?"

"October. That's a good time, isn't it? You know, autumn in New York."

He sang the song's opening phrase into the phone, and she laughed quietly. He felt warm and close to her.

"How's Mojo?'

"Missing you."

"How about his master? Are you missing me?"

"You don't know how much." Buddy realized that he hadn't known how much until now.

"I'll be home tomorrow and you can show me how much."

"My pleasure."

"Buddy, Art called me and told me about Eldon being murdered."

"What's that son of a bitch doing callin' you? How'd he know where you were staying?'

"I don't know. Called around until he found me, I guess."

"The hell with this!" Buddy slammed the phone onto its cradle. Anger rushed him so hard that he picked up his half full coffee mug and pulled back his arm to add force to the blow as he thrust the mug into the sink. Ceramic shattered against the porcelain basin and the sound of it breaking calmed him a little, taking some of his anger with it. There was a knock on the door and he walked over to yank it open, expecting Justin and Mojo back from the park. That fresh smell of soap met him.

"Buddy," Carolyn said. "It's me."

He turned and went back into the kitchen. She followed.

"Buddy, you know I couldn't say anything yesterday. You have to understand."

"I understand. You were just playing around."

"Buddy."

He heard the pleading edge to her voice and it fueled the anger inside him again. He was stupid to get involved with a cop. She was his friend's woman and they both knew they had betrayed his trust. The night they spent together had been a selfish act, a careless thing really. He was through with it now. Through with her.

"Go on back to work or where you were headed, Carolyn. I'll keep your secret. I like John Allen too much not to."

He could feel her fingers on his arm and he pulled away. "Get out now. Leave me alone."

She took a step away, and then stopped. There was the fresh smell and movement of air as she walked into the kitchen. "There's glass on the floor. Did you break something? A cup?"

"Let it go."

"I'll clean it up." He heard cabinet doors opening. "You're barefoot."

"I'll put on shoes."

He heard the swish of a broom across the floor; the clink of glass into the garbage and water running in the sink. Down the drain, he thought, just like the hours and passion they shared just two nights ago.

"I won't let them charge you. I'll tell them before it comes to that." She was at his side again, her hand touching his.

"Forget it, Carolyn. I'll be fine." Then, because he knew it would diminish her, he added, "It would hurt Ivy if she found out. I wouldn't want her to know we had a one night stand."

Carolyn withdrew her hand as if his had suddenly turned to fire. She walked to the door and left without another word, the door clicking shut behind her.

He sat down at the piano and played *Jolie Blon* over and over. His mind danced with Yvette as she moved across the floor, full skirt swirling about her bare legs, the scent of sandalwood following her, the taste of gin in her kiss. A knock interrupted him and he opened the door without asking who it was.

"It's John Allen, Buddy. Can I come in?"

"Sure. But you need to understand that I have a lawyer now."

"This is off the record."

"Have a seat if you want." Buddy went into the living room and leaned against the sofa arm, half sitting, half standing.

Allen's voice came from the direction of the chair. "I've been to Louie's and asked around. Seems you left something out of your story. Folks tell me you were with a woman cop. You were there with Carolyn, weren't you?"

"Yeah. She took me over to see Jimmy in the hospital so I bought her dinner. Seemed like the right thing to do."

"Where'd you go after dinner?"

"What's the problem, man?" Buddy could make out the outline of Allen leaning forward in the chair. "We had dinner."

"It's not dinner that concerns me."

"You thinking it's something more, let it go," Buddy said, the lie coming easy. "I went to Amos' place that night. We worked on some new songs."

"You didn't tell anyone that when they questioned you yesterday."

"They had already made me for the murder so I felt I needed a lawyer. I didn't want to get Carolyn involved, just because of what you're thinking right now. Call Amos, he'll put you straight."

"We'll call Amos alright." Allen was standing now. "Heard they confiscated your blade."

"Gave it to Miller yesterday."

Allen moved closer to Buddy and took his hand. Buddy could feel the slender casing of a switchblade knife as Allen wrapped Buddy's hand around it.

"Someone thinks you have their drugs. They'll be coming after you and you'll need this," Allen said. "Be careful."

A blast of hot air came in as the door opened and Mojo, smelling like earth and grass, came rushing up to rub against Buddy's leg.

"Got to get to class," Justin said, his voice fading as ran down the walkway. "Catch you later."

"I'm leaving now, too," Allen said. "Anyone asks, I was never here."

After they were gone, Buddy sat on the floor with Mojo resting against him; the house quiet except for the sound of Chet Baker's trumpet floating out from the radio in the bedroom. Buddy ran his fingers over the smooth, narrow knife in his hands. It wasn't the knife he had turned over to the detective yesterday, but it was sleek and deadly, a street fighters' weapon of choice. Since he was fifteen and part of a street gang, he had carried one like this in his pocket. He pushed the button and a blade sprang from its case with lightening speed. Touching the edge, he felt the metal's sharpness against his palm. Buddy wasn't sure why Allen had given it to him. Allen did not seemed convinced that nothing happened between Buddy and Carolyn. Yet, Allen was his friend and he believed someone wanted to kill Buddy.

"Someone will come for you," he heard Allen say.

Let them come.

Chapter Thirty-Three

Near supper time, Amos and Strum came over to work on a new song Amos had written, called "Annie's Gone."

Strum called and said they were coming, that they wanted to get the song ready for the gig next week. "We need to work this out, Buddy. Amos wants it in the lineup."

Buddy hesitated. He needed to be alone tonight. He said, "Let's do it early. I'm pretty tired."

They ordered Chinese take out and ate in the kitchen, talking over the new arrangement where Amos would take the lead. Buddy knew the composition was a personal kind of grieving for Amos. The handsome, smiling guitar player had women around him after every gig, all vying for his attention. But a couple of years ago he had fallen hard for an Asian student attending college in Louisiana. Her name was Annie.

Ivy told Buddy that Annie was a small woman with eyes black as onyx and the kind of smile that stayed on her lips and never traveled across her face, so you never knew what she was thinking. Buddy remembered that Annie had rarely joined the conversation when the band members met after a gig or for a barbecue. She had never been part of the lighthearted chatter they kept up backstage before a show.

Annie was offhanded in the way she treated Amos, and for reasons the rest of them never understood, he was crazy about her. The day she left Louisiana and flew back to Japan, Amos disappeared for a week. It was months before that infectious laugh returned and his guitar playing recovered the genius he'd shown before Annie.

Buddy thought that the separation of a year and half a world would have made Amos give up on a memory that lived only in his solitude. But here he was with this sad song tailor made for the blues. It was a hellva tune, Buddy had to admit, so maybe something good had come from the whole mess. Still, Buddy was restless as they went over the arrangement, starting and stopping for what seemed an endless amount of times.

"Gettin' close to midnight," Strum declared, standing up and moving across the room. "I need to get on home. "My Ruthie swore she's gonna change the door clocks if I don't spend more time there."

"Me too," Amos said. "I want to catch the last set over at the Night Cat. Maybe I'll take that little cocktail waitress home after closing."

Buddy felt some relief hearing the click of locks snapping shut on guitar cases as the two prepared to leave. Strum slapped him on the shoulder and Amos touched his hand.

"You be alright here tonight?"

"Yeah, I'm okay," Buddy answered. "Ivy'll be back tomorrow."

As soon as he heard their voices fading down the sidewalk, Buddy closed the door and left it unlocked. It had been nagging at him all evening, a feeling that this whole thing was ready for some kind of showdown.

It has to be tonight, he thought, before Ivy comes home.

He walked to the bedroom and opened the sliding door to the patio, stepping out into the night. He felt along the outside wall with the palms of his hands, sliding along the surface, the stucco rough against his skin. There was the smell of jasmine and the call of a night bird as he inched along, the cool of evening setting in after the scorching summer day. He touched a medal cover, found the latch and opened the box. His fingers touched switches lined in a neat row until he found the main circuit breaker. He flipped the switches down, one by one. He closed the cover and went back into the house, pushing the door shut behind him.

In the living room again, he settled into the overstuffed chair and Mojo dropped to lie at his feet. The house was quiet, without the familiar, faint sounds of jazz trailing from the bedroom, or the insistent hum of a refrigerator.

Buddy took the knife from his pocket and felt the smooth, cool surface in his hand. He pushed the button so the blade sprang forth like a striking cobra. He waited in the dark silence.

It could have been an hour or several hours that he sat there thinking of Yvette brushing her fingers through his curls or laughing for no other reason except the joy of the moment; of Ivy and him, sitting together on the piano bench, singing some old show tune; remembering Jimmy telling him he had a wild Irish heart.

Hazy reflections moved in his mind of boys fighting on a grassy battlefield. The motorcycle chain in the hands of a youthful warrior as it made the air suck, moving swiftly toward his head, police sirens wailing in the distance. He never felt the blow that changed his life and brought him to this moment.

He waited as time inched by, his mind assembling the puzzle pieces of his life.

He waited, because he knew someone would be coming.

Mojo moved beside him, suddenly alert.

The door creaked open in increments and Mojo growled deep in his throat. Buddy touched the dog, silencing him. The door clicked shut. There was a soft footstep and then hesitation as Mojo growled another warning.

"You know me, Mojo," a man whispered. "Quiet now."

"No need to whisper, Rufus. I've been waiting for you."

If Rufus was startled, he made no sound. He just stood where he was for a moment. "Where are you? You in that big chair ain't you?" he said. "Where's the dog?"

"We're right here."

"Just give me my stuff, Buddy, and I'm gone."

"You already know its not here. You tore the place apart looking for it."

"We'll have a drink, talk it over," Rufus' voice became reasonable, cajoling. "Tell me where you stashed it."

Buddy could feel Rufus move across the floor. Mojo got to his feet, but Buddy held on to him. The light switch clicked.

"No lights, Rufus. Welcome to my world. We're both doing this in the dark."

"You son-of-a-bitch. That won't stop me."

"Why'd you kill Nina, Rufus? She was harmless."

"Stupid junkie, she had it coming." Rufus laughed. "Wanted to stay high but never had any scratch to pay. Threatened to drop a dime on me."

"The others too?"

"Washington was holding out on me, and Eldon, that poor greedy bastard, wanted a bigger cut. Said he was gonna tell you the whole story, 'bout how we was using you for a mule."

"An ice pick for God's sake."

"It's quick and quiet. You'll find out."

"Kill me or not, Rufus, the cops' got your stash."

"You always was a fool, you blind bastard. You got talent, but you jes throw it away on booze and women."

Buddy stood up. "I know this house like the back of my hand, Rufus. Come on and get me."

Rufus was treading lightly across the floor; Buddy could feel the vibration of his steps as he came toward him. The dark, silent house seemed to anticipate, as Buddy did, the approach of danger. Mojo bristled beneath Buddy's hand and his growl grew louder.

Buddy moved in slow motion away from the chair, backing toward a corner where the shadows were even deeper in the blackness. Rufus laughed and Buddy could make out a small beam of light finding its way across the room. So Rufus had a flashlight, Buddy realized.

Buddy found the window drapes and concealed himself behind one. He could make out the light as it moved across the room in a single, round glare. Rufus stepped across the carpet, searching with his pinpoint of light. He grew closer to the window where Buddy waited.

"Get 'em!" Buddy commanded and released Mojo.

The dog sprang from the floor, bounding upward, his growl a snarl now, hurling the force of his weight against Rufus who screamed in surprise.

The yip of pain from Mojo was followed by a thud as the dog dropped to the floor.

The ice pick! Oh God! No! It took all the control Buddy could muster to stay put.

The fuzzy light disappeared. Rufus no longer had the flashlight. He must have dropped it when Mojo attacked. Buddy could smell the sweat, blood and fear that came with Rufus as he moved closer.

Buddy gripped the handle of the knife. Just a little closer. A step or two more.

"I kilt yo dog," Rufus snickered. "Used my ice pick. But I pulled it out so's I could use it on his boss too."

Buddy could feel him now, standing near enough to touch. In one swift movement, he stepped out beside him and plunged the blade into soft flesh. The knife twisted in Buddy's hand as Rufus spun around, cursing. Buddy pulled his knife free and put up his left hand as he felt something coming toward him. Something went completely through the palm of his hand and out again. The ice pick!

A second blow and searing pain made Buddy stagger. The point of Rufus' ice pick was buried in his shoulder. Buddy thrust his knife into

Rufus again, their bodies so close they were touching. Buddy could feel the splatter of blood against his face.

"Oh Jesus!" Rufus moaned.

One thump, then another as Rufus went down. Maybe he hit the table as he fell, Buddy thought, as he heard a crash an another thump. Buddy moved toward the sound and stumbled against Rufus' body.

"I hope I killed the bastard."

Buddy wanted to get to Mojo, to help him. Maybe the dog wasn't dead.

"Mojo!" he called and heard a low, weak whine.

Buddy moved in a disoriented stagger across the room. Bumping into the counter, he fumbled over the surface until he found the phone. His left hand was useless so he clutched the receiver with his right, his shoulder racked with pain and warm blood trailed down his arm onto the cradle as he pushed the buttons. An operator was asking what his emergency was. His legs buckled under him and he fell to his knees.

Chapter Thirty-Four

She was whispering a song; a faint, distant melody that called him to consciousness. Her long, slender fingers were covering his, and a light, sweet gardenia scent told him that Ivy was there, crooning something close to a lullaby in an almost inaudible voice.

He called out and she soothed him. But the movie replayed in his mind, over and over, like a flickering film. He and Rufus met in the dark and struggled for survival. There was the smell of fear on both of them as their blood smeared together. Close as an embrace, their bodies touched, each trying to destroy the other. With an ice pick buried in his shoulder, the searing pain ripping through him, Buddy had dug a knife into Rufus with all his might, feeling it slide somewhere into a hard body.

It was hazy now, but he remembered kneeling on the carpet because his legs refused to hold him, his knees digging hard in the soft pile as he fought to stay lucid.

"I think I killed him," he said into the phone.

He remembered a crash; He remmembered a crash; the door being kicked open and Carolyn yelling.

"Buddy? Are you here? Where are you? What's wrong with the goddamn lights?"

"Mojo," Buddy whispered as he felt Allen's arms around him. "Help Mojo."

A jarring ride in an ambulance, a siren wailing as it sped through the city streets. Then blackness.

"Ivy." He tried to move, but he seemed to be tied down with tubes and wires and a piercing pain in his left shoulder.

"I'm here, darling."

"Mojo?"

"He'll be okay; the ice pick missed any vital organs. He's in the vet hospital."

"Rufus?"

"He's dead." Ivy's fingers tightened around his. "Police aren't charging you with anything."

"He told me he killed Nina." Pain stabbed at Buddy's arm. "How bad is my shoulder?"

"Doctor said it will heal. So will your hand, but you won't be playing the guitar for a while." Ivy gave a teasing little laugh. "We'll just have to listen to you sing."

They were quiet for a minute. Two nurses stopped outside the room to talk and laughter came from down the hall.

"Jimmy was here earlier," Ivy said.

"He okay now?" Buddy's lips were dry and he wanted to ease the persistent throb in his shoulder and an ache in his left hand.

"He's pretty good. I tried to get him to come home with me but he wouldn't."

"Ivy, ask them to give me a shot or something."

"Just push this button. It's a drip."

"Got Jack in it?"

"Even better than Jack," she said and laughed. But it did not hide the note of concern in her voice.

Chapter Thirty-Five

Clad only in a pair of old jeans, Buddy sat on the floor of the condo, leaning against the sofa and fingering the frets on the Gibson, the music floating in his mind. Mojo lay stretched out against his leg. It was almost two months now since Buddy had played a note. His hands were still stiff but the pain was gone. A little practice, he thought, and he'd be back where he was before Rufus stuck an ice pick in his hand and shoulder.

Last two gigs with the band he had sung, leaving the guitar playing to Amos and Strum. But the fans wanted him to play, and he needed to play, so with some effort, he expected to be in shape on Saturday night.

Ivy slid down the sofa onto the floor beside Buddy, pressing against him. The feel of her slender body, the cloud of her perfume and the silk of her hair distracted Buddy from the guitar.

"Hey baby," he said.

"Hey to you," she answered. "How's your hand?"

"Little more practice and I'll play again."

"I'm working on a deal for a week in Las Vegas."

"The boys will like that. Are we headlining?"

"Don't know yet. We're okay money wise so you can take some time off." She ran a finger down the scar on his cheek. "Maybe stay there a few days after the booking."

"No."

"Can we talk about it?"

"No."

"A honeymoon, maybe, while we are there."

Buddy pulled a pick across the guitar strings. "Have to be married for that."

"Don't you think it's time, Buddy?" We've been together since we were sixteen."

Buddy put the instrument on the floor and turned in her direction. "What the hell's this about Ivy? Suddenly we need to be married?"

"Fifteen years is suddenly?"

"This got anything to do with Art Kimble? I know he's been calling you."

She pulled away from him. "How many times do I have to say that I'm not interested in Art?"

"Maybe you need to tell him that."

Mojo got to his feet as Ivy stood up. "I'm thirty years old. I've given you half my life and now I want to be married. Make up your mind."

"Or what?"

"Or maybe next time you decide to wallow in the gutter some one else will have to pull you out." Ivy walked away and Mojo followed. Buddy heard the bedroom door slam.

Buddy tugged at the gold loop in his ear. Every so often Ivy started talking about marriage. Sometimes she would say how she needed to have a kid before her clock ran out. He would tell her that he was a blind blues musician who worked nights and weekends in an eight to five world. Every gig could be his last in the insecure, unconventional world of blues music, and he didn't know how to be anything else.

Buddy knew he didn't want to be without Ivy, but his pride would not let him give in. Belonging to someone, the way he had belonged to Yvette, inhaling their every move until you need them to breathe, watching them leave long before you could let go, was not something he ever wanted to experience again. Marry Ivy or lose her was not a choice his pride would let him make.

She was in the bedroom now, he knew, holding onto Mojo for comfort, crying into the dog's dark fur, maybe hoping he would come in and say it was alright, they would get married in Vegas. Maybe something inside Buddy wanted to do that, but he didn't move from his place on the floor.

**

The motel manager unlocked the door and stepped aside. He had the clipped accent of someone from the Middle East. There was a faint smell of curry under a strong sent of Bay Rum. "How long are you planning to stay?"

"Few days, maybe a week," Buddy answered. A warm September breeze promised rain as it swept past the open door.

"I'll just leave the key on this table," the man said. "You have some luggage?"

"Lot of baggage. No luggage."

"What?"

"Never mind." Buddy put the brown pizza box on the table. "You have room service don't you?"

"Oh yes, sir. Our kitchen is open until 10 p.m." The manager hesitated. "Can you use the phone?"

"I can push a button."

"The dog—he will need to go out?"

"This room have a patio?"

"Sliding glass door leads out to the common area. I can show you." He stopped as if embarrassed. "Someone will have to clean up." Buddy took a hundred dollar bill from his pocket, touching the folds to make sure of the denomination, and handed it to the man. "If someone can help with that, we'll be fine. Can I get someone to make a run to the liquor store? Couple of fifths of Jack Daniels, black label. Keep the change."

"Yes, sir." The door closed behind him, shutting off the breeze. The air conditioner chilled the room and heavy drapes muffled the outside noise. Buddy found the radio and turned the knob, searching for a blues station. He found KBLZ and heard Art Kimble's voice blast into the room.

Buddy kicked off his shoes and unbuttoned his shirt. Every motel seemed to have that used smell of hundreds of travelers journeying through. Every room was home to strangers for one night or more; until they moved on as if they had never been there. Buddy felt his way into the bathroom and ran several inches of water into the tub.

"In case you get thirsty," he said to Mojo.

By the time he got back into the bedroom and pushed the patio door open just enough for Mojo to fit through, there was a knock at the door.

"Yeah?"

"Your delivery, sir." It was a different, younger voice than the one of the man he asked to bring him a bottle.

Buddy opened the door part way and stood in the frame.

"Say, ain't you that guitar player; that blues guy?" the voice said. "You got a hit song out now. Number one on the charts or something."

"Number two."

Buddy took the paper bag and started to shut the door but a hand held it open.

"You want me to get you something to mix that with?" the kid said. "I can bring you some ice and 7Up or Coke from the machine."

"No thanks. I don't want to bruise it." Buddy shut the door.

He pulled the bottles of Jack Daniels free, letting the sack drop to the floor. Plumping the pillows up against the headboard, he settled on the bed and unscrewed the lid of one of the whiskey bottles.

"Hello old friend," he said to the bewitching brew as he raised the container to his lips.

Just the two of them, the way he liked it, spending some time together in that dark place where memories and demons danced on the perimeters but kept their distance like wild animals from a roaring campfire. He would fill the hole in his soul one more time.

It was six weeks now since they had released him from the hospital and he had waited for this moment. He knew that in a day or two Strum would come looking for him. Ivy would call all motels in Baton Rouge until she found him. Jimmy would take Buddy in and put him in his old bedroom with the Eric Clapton poster on the wall and nurse him the way he had Yvette before the gin finally took her completely.

Ivy would cry and Buddy would promise to stay sober. And he would for a while.

He drank deeply from the fifth, the liquid already fire in his veins, his mind at ease. Over the radio, Art's voice came into the room.

"Number two on the charts, a song catching a lot of attention, played by a local group. Give a listen to *Last Call* by Blind Buddy and Mojo's Blues Band."

Buddy smiled with satisfaction. It was where he wanted to be, with his song on top, his name up with the blues icons. Wasn't it? There was Buddy's guitar riff in the high register and then his voice with its low gravelly texture. *Last Call*, he sang, *Baby, it's the last call---.*

He paused with the bottle almost to his lips and sang with his recorded voice. *"Last call, it will be my last call..."*

He smiled. Maybe not the last.

Chapter Thirty-Six

Mojo was barking, the sound filling the room, jarring Buddy awake.

"It's okay, boy, we're going take you home," a voice said.

Buddy tried to lift his head, but he couldn't move. The air was humid under the swish of a ceiling fan above the bed where he lay. An old blues tune was playing somewhere; maybe the radio. He opened his eyes and made out shadows moving in a heavy fog. Mojo stopped barking and began to whine.

"Help me get him on his feet." It was Amos talking. Buddy recognized him now.

"Damn, it stinks in here." Buddy knew that was Strum's voice.

"I want him out of here," another man said. "Good thing you men came, 'cause I was gonna call the cops."

"Just cool it, man. He owe you any money?" Strum asked.

"Well, the room's a mess."

"Here's fifty," Amos said. "That work for you?"

"Just take him and that dog outa here."

"You go on, we'll get him," Strum said.

The music stopped and a breeze came from somewhere, maybe an open door. God! Buddy's head hurt.

"Should we put him in the shower?"

"Naw, let's jes' take him like he is."

"Why you think he did this, Strum? Got a song number one on the charts. Why'd he do it?"

"The way he is, Amos. The way he's been since I known him. The itch comes on him, he got to scratch it."

"If I had a woman like Ivy, I'd been afraid of losing her."

"She's part of the problem 'cause whe puts up with it. Help me get him up on his feet."

One on each side, they were pulling him off the bed. They put his limp arms over their shoulders and dragged him across the carpet toward the breeze. He thought he might throw up, the bile rising with each step.

Mojo growled as they pulled him along.

"We ain't hurtin' him, Mojo," Strum said. "We takin' him home."

"You think he needs to go to the hospital?" Amos asked.

"Nope. That would makes the news and we don't want the whole world knowing he's a binge drunk," Strum answered. "It's our band we're talking about. Don't need no bad pubilicy."

"We carryin' him to Jimmy's or on home to Ivy? Hate for her to see him looking like this."

"Could be she needs to see him looking like a street wino." Strum sounded disgusted. "Know how many times I've done this?"

"But you keep on."

"I love the cat. He's the best damn bluesman I ever seen."

Buddy tried to speak but the words strangled in his throat. They were dragging him across pavement now, his bare feet scraping cement. They threw him in the backseat of a car, and he lay face up, his arm hanging on the floor, Mojo's furry body rubbing against him.

The motion of the car churned Buddy's stomach and he fought to keep vomit away. His head felt as if it was split in two and his entire body was trembling. Mojo licked his face in sympathy.

"Give me a drink," Buddy managed to croak. But no one answered.

Mercifully, the car stopped and he was pulled from the backseat. He threw up, leaning forward, bending almost double.

"Shit!" Amos said. "Just missed me."

They were pulling him again, across grass now. They stopped and held him, knocking on a door. The sound was like a wrecking ball in his head. When the door opened, there was faint music from a jazz quartet and the smell of gardenias.

"Thank God! You found him," he heard Ivy say. She touched his face. "Take him in the bedroom."

"Which one?" Amos said. "You don't want him in your bed like this. Where's the bathtub? We'll clean him up some."

They dragged Buddy some more, across carpet and tile and then lowered him into a tub, the porcelain cool against his skin. Hands yanked and pulled at his clothes until he lay naked, holding his arm around his head protectively. The cold water spraying down on him jolted him upright but it seemed as if an octopus was holding him with tentacles of iron. Shampoo and soap ran from his hair down his face and his body as water came from above and filled the tub where he sat. He felt like he was drowning in an onslaught of water from everywhere..

Mercifully it stopped and they lifted him up, rubbed him down like a Chevrolet in a car wash, and pushed him onto a bed. The torture was over for now.

"You go on Strum, I'll sit here for a while. Make sure he don't try to leave," Amos said.

"Suits me." Strum answered. "Call me if you need a ride back to your place."

**

Buddy stirred and sat up, his head pounding. He was pretty sure Ivy was there because of the shadowy figure and light fragrance near him.

She touched his arm. "Here, take these aspirins. There's 7up in this glass."

"Thanks, baby." Buddy swallowed the tablets and washed them down with the bubbling liquid. "Is Mojo okay?"

"He's fine. Half starved, but fine."

"Sorry, Ivy, I—"

She cut him off, "I'm leaving you, Buddy. I'm going to Jan's place for a while. I'll let you know where I am after that."

Buddy felt for the bedside table and put the glass on it. "What are you talking about?"

"It's my last trip to the gutter and back. Told you that last time, but you didn't listen. I'm just through waiting for you."

"Ivy." It was all he could say. Who was she, this woman with steel in her voice and ice in her touch? "You don't mean that."

He struggled to his feet, feeling weak and reaching out for something to hold onto, his hands catching only air.

"Oh, yes, this time I do mean it. You're in the spare bedroom," she said. "If you can get dressed and find your way into the kitchen there's some food on the table for you. Your clothes are on the chair to your left."

"Baby, you can't—" he began, but the door closed behind her.

Buddy pulled on the jeans he found folded on the chair, leaving the shirt and shoes, not taking time to put them on. He made his way to the door and into the kitchen. Mojo rubbed against him as he walked and he reached down to pat the dog's head.

"Ivy, let's talk about this," Buddy said.

"I'm all out of words. I've decided to call Henry and see if he and I can join up again to do some gigs like we did before. I'm a jazz singer and that's what I plan to do."

"Okay, well that's what we agreed, that you would get back to that as soon as the album was released."

He grabbed her and pulled her to him. She did not resist, but stood like a statue, so close to him that he could feel her body warmth.

"You don't have to leave to do that," he said.

"I have to leave because I'm tired of wanting it to be my turn. Tired of wanting you to sober up, of wanting you to want to marry me, tired of wanting what I want to matter."

"Where did all this anger come from? I thought we were in this together, that you loved me."

"I've always loved you Buddy. I've been waiting for you to love me back."

"You're every breath I take," he tried to nuzzle her neck but she pulled back.

"Pretty words, Buddy. They're just lyrics to a song." Her voice cracked. "From now on you can make love to that guitar, that's really all you care about."

Buddy let go of her arm and sunk onto a hardback chair at the table. "When are you going?"

"Now," she said. "It's best. Maybe we can do this without all the drama."

Maybe he really didn't want to know, but he had to ask anyway. "Does this have anything to do with Art Kimble?"

"The person I'm leaving you for is me, Ivy Martin. Who the hell am I anyway? I plan to find out."

"Listen, this is really your place, I can go crash at Jimmy's. You stay here."

"No," she said. "I can't be here at all. I want to somewhere without memories; without the smell and feel of you all around me."

Buddy put his elbows on the table and rested his head on his hands. "I love you, baby. I always have, always will."

"Amos was here until a couple of hours ago," she said as if she had not heard him. "We talked about everything. I told him my plans and all. I gave him the information on the bookings I set up, including the ones in New York."

She touched the curls on the top of his head. "Goodbye Buddy."

His pride faltered. "What'll I do without you?"

"You'll be fine."

Don't let it hurt, he told himself, don't let her see. "Sure, I will baby. You do what you got to do."

Buddy heard Mojo whining, heard Ivy whispering in the dog's fur and heard the door click shut behind her.

Buddy's hands began to shake. He really needed the comfort of his old friend Jack Daniels; needed to return to that sweet oblivion where the world waited outside the walled gates, unable to enter the magic kingdom. He made his hands into fists and held them against the table to stop the trembling.

"I'll be fine," he yelled out the words and they vibrated off the walls. "Yeah, I'll be fine. You know I'll be fine."

Mojo whimpered and put his nose on Buddy's knee. Buddy dropped his head back onto his hands.

Something was missing, he realized, something that was always there, something he took for granted. No sound flowed from the bedroom.

The music was gone.

Chapter Thirty-Seven

"What's this?" Jan asked, eyeing the two bags at Ivy's feet. "You goin' somewhere?"

"I need a place to stay for a while." Ivy pushed the luggage inside the door as Jan stepped aside.

"You leaving him?" Jan shut the door behind her younger sister. "What'd he do, go on another drunk?"

"Yes, but its more than that." Ivy sank down on an overstuffed chair. "I feel like he'll use me up if I stay. There'll be nothing left of me."

Jan patted her on the shoulder. "Sure, you can camp out here. No problem."

She walked into the kitchen, took two wine glasses from the overhead rack and placed them on the counter. "He know you're gone?"

"Of course. I wouldn't have left otherwise."

Jan opened the refrigerator, took out a half full bottle of white wine and pulled the cork. She filled the glasses and brought them back into the living room, handing one to Ivy.

"How'd he take it?"

"You know Buddy." Ivy accepted the glass and held it without giving it any attention. People always offered a glass of wine or cup of tea as if it would cure a broken heart or a ruined life.

Jan drank from her glass. "Just let you go? Didn't beg you to stay?"

"He'd never do that." But in her mind, Ivy remembered Buddy asking what he would do without her.

Jan sat down and crossed her legs. She held the wine glass in one hand, resting it on her knee. Ivy thought Jan was beautiful. She was a tall, dark-haired woman with dark blue eyes that hinted at the impulsive nature she lived by. She did not look like Ivy except for an occasional mannerism or expression or laugh. Three years apart in age, they shared a mother, but different fathers. Their mother had married five times, improving her financial lot with each husband. Growing up, the girls were often left to their own resources and Ivy depended on Jan when their mother was off on some new adventure with a new man. To Ivy, she and Jan were bound to each other by love as well as blood. More than sisters, to Ivy they were best friends.

"Look, honey, you know I love Buddy," Jan said. "He's just about the sexiest thing I've ever seen, in a brooding sort of James Dean way. But he doesn't treat you right."

"He still has a lot of anger about his mother's death and his blindness. Now this thing with his drummer," Ivy realized she was defending Buddy again.

"You going to stay away?" Jan asked.

Determination, however temporary, steadied Ivy. "I'm going to call Henry, you remember him, my piano player? I'll see if I can get us some work."

"You're not going back to the insurance company?"

"Not yet. I'm still on leave." Ivy lifted the glass and sipped the wine. "I'll see how it goes."

Jan smiled and raised her eyebrows as if she did not believe Ivy's resolve. "Remember that song you sing about love being a cold, rainy day?" she said.

"Yeah, I guess that's it all right," Ivy said and smiled. "My whole life is a sad little song."

Jan set her glass on the coffee table and stood up. "I'll clean my stuff off the bed in the spare room. It's yours as long as you need it."

**

It wasn't so bad, Ivy told herself, living with Jan. An attendant with a trans-world airline, Jan was gone for days at a time. When she wasn't working, Jan might run off for a weekend in some exotic place with only hours notice, or go to a party and return a day or two later.

"Come with me, Ivy," she urged. "Get lost in the now."

"That's your way, not mine," Ivy would answer.

Henry, who had accompanied Ivy when she sang for the last two years, was happy to get back to work. He was a man in his late thirties with a wife and a new baby. His day job as a manager at a print shop paid the bills, but he was a musician at heart. She and Henry rehearsed their old songbook and were able to get booked into a hotel lounge right away. The small jazz clubs, so popular in the 1940s and 50s had all but faded into musical history and work for a singer like Ivy was hard to come by.

When Jan was away Ivy was restless. She would read the same page of a novel over and over, never remembering what she had read. She was constantly flipping the television channels because she couldn't make sense of the shows and she was unable to concentrate in conversations, even with people she knew well. Art Kimble left messages on her voice mail, but she never returned his calls. A dozen times a day she wondered if Buddy was getting to rehearsals or if he made the gig she had booked for the band. Many times she opened her phone to call Buddy, and then stopped. She reached for him in the night but touched only the cool cotton sheet. Once she called Amos, but when the call went to his voice mail she hung up without leaving a message.

If I'm looking for Ivy Martin, she thought, I need to start the search. It seemed to her that she was nobody with Buddy and nobody without him.

The two weeks she had been gone from Buddy seemed like forever. But her first night in the hotel cocktail lounge made her feel whole again, doing the kind of music she believed she was meant to do.

The spotlight fell on Ivy as she leaned against the baby grand piano and Henry played an introduction to *My Funny Valentine*. She started the song in a quiet, smoky voice, meaning every word, bending every phrase. Her long, black dress was slit up the side almost to her thigh and it opened as she stepped away from the piano, flashing her bare leg. She scanned the audience, as she knew she would every night, but Buddy was not there. Why did she think he would be?

Art came in half way through the set. He settled on a bar stool and ordered a drink. Dressed in pleated tan slacks and a brown silk shirt, he was too smooth, too confident, and too handsome.

She finished the song and Henry said into the microphone, "Ivy has a song climbing the charts right now; looking like it might reach the number one slot. Maybe we can get her to sing *Last Call* for us right now."

The audience applauded encouragement and Ivy shot Henry a look of frustration, but he had already begun the introduction. She started the song and Art raised his glass to her in salute. After the set, she walked over to the bar where he waited.

"I ordered you a chardonnay" he said. "You sound wonderful."

"Thanks." She sat on the barstool next to him.

"You didn't return my calls?" he said as if it were a misunderstanding.

"I thought it best not to." The bartender placed the wine glass in front of her and she touched the stem with her fingertips. The glass was cold and damp with moisture that formed on the outside.

"Let's have supper after the show," Art said.

"No, I don't think so."

He placed his hand on her wrist. "I really want to see you. It's just supper."

"No. It doesn't feel right, not now." She raised the glass to her lips and drank.

"We'd be so good together," Art said.

Henry ran the scales on the piano, signaling for her to return to the stage. Ivy slid off the stool and removed Art's hand from her arm.

"You don't need me."

He stayed through the next song and when she looked again, Art was gone. She felt relieved.

The audience was thin, with a few singles at the bar and some couples at the tables, leaning towards each other and talking, not listening to her. She ended the evening with *Sunday Kind of Love*. There was scattered applause as she said goodnight and left the stage.

"Want me to walk to you to your car, Ivy?" Henry asked.

"No, I'm going to change out of this dress into some street clothes before I leave. Jan might have a houseful of people when I get there." She could not call it home, not yet.

"I need to get home, the baby wakes up at all hours and Kay needs my help," Henry said. "No one prepared us for all the work a new baby is."

"You go on, I'll be fine," Ivy said. "My car's in the hotel parking garage so I feel safe enough."

"Goodnight, then." Henry kissed her cheek and walked across the lounge with Ivy's arrangements in a binder under his arm. Ivy went into the employee's break room and changed her clothes in the bathroom attached to it. She hung her dress on a hanger and placed a plastic cover over it, took off her high heels and tossed them in the bottom of the dress bag and zipped it shut. Then she slid into a pair of jeans, a cotton blouse and sandals. She pulled her hair back and fastened an elastic band around it and washed her face in the sink. Looking forward to Jan's sofa, a bowl of cereal and an old movie on television, she put the dress bag over her arm, slung her large purse over one shoulder and left the hotel by the side door that opened into the parking garage.

The heat assaulted her as she walked out of the air conditioned hotel into the cement structure smelling of oil, dirt and tire rubber. She found her car, clicked the locks and opened the back door, placing the gown bag on the seat. In the next terrifying moment she felt someone grab her from behind, shove her into the car and jump in with her.

Ivy felt the sting of metal scraping her fingers as her keys were ripped from her hand and tossed over the seat to a second man leaping in behind the wheel.

"Go! Go!" the man holding her yelled, slamming the car door.

Chapter Thirty-Eight

"What's the matter with you tonight? You were way off," Strum said. "Amos was carrying the whole load."

Buddy slid his guitar into its case and said nothing. He knew Strum was right, that he couldn't seem to put any heart into his music, that his playing was flat lining, throwing the entire band off. His performance has been a cliché. He knew Ivy was singing over at the hotel tonight, that's where his mind was, wishing he was there listening to her.

"You got a way home? 'Cause I'm leaving," Strum said, irritation in his voice.

"Yeah, I got him," Amos said. "I need just a minute to make sure Liz is still on the menu, soon as she clocks out. Wait here Buddy, I'll be right back."

Billy John, the new drummer, was dropping his symbols in their place, laughing with Franklin over some inside joke while he worked disassembling his drums. Franklin had brought Billy John to audition for Buddy and fill the spot Rufus had left. While Billy John did not have the hard drive of Rufus, he had an amazing way of anticipating what Buddy would do next, as if he could read his musical mind and stayed one step ahead.

"You don't need us, Buddy, we're goin' now. Try to catch the last show at the Kat Klub," Franklin said.

Buddy smiled. "You're daddy know you go there?"

"Naw, some things he's better off not knowing."

"Go on then. Amos will carry me home."

They left and Buddy felt the sudden silence around him. He reached down to touch Mojo for reassurance. He wondered if Ivy was finished with her set, wondered what songs she had done, wondered if she looked in the audience for him, if she wished he was there. Then Mojo's whine let them know they were not alone.

"O'Brian," a voice said from a few feet away, probably at the far edge of the stage, near the entry. "We figure you still owe us something."

"Who the hell are you?"

"Rufus was my cousin. You remember Rufus? You kilt him."

Buddy's hand went into his pocket and closed around the knife. "Whatta ya want?"

"Besides killing my blood kin, you took our dope. After I built that great place in your RV, too."

"I gave the stuff to the cops. You know that." Buddy could identify the voice; he recognized it as the carjacker who wanted to break his hands.

"Yeah, I know. But that don't make us even. Figure you still owe us. We'll settle the debt for five hundred grand." The voice laughed. "Put it in a guitar case."

"You're full of shit. That's half a million. I don't have that kind of cash." Buddy tightened his grip on the knife. Mojo was moving beside him and growling low in his throat.

"How much is your little canary girlfriend worth to you?"

"You son of a bitch!"

"You think about it."

" What's your name?"

"Five hundred large, by noon at the Good Night Motel. Come in a taxi so we can see that you be alone."

"You saying you got Ivy?"

"Oh yeah, and leave that damn dog at home."

"Where is she?"

The voice was gone.

"Okay, we're all set." Amos said as came up behind Buddy. "Who you talking to?"

Buddy forced himself calm. "Nobody. Just Mojo."

"Well, let me get you on home then. I got a promise waitin' for me. Liz gonna ride along with us."

Buddy and Mojo sat in the back seat of Amos's car, Buddy paying no attention to the small talk going on between Amos and Liz in the front. The ride seemed to last forever and Buddy's mind whirled with what actions he should take. Did they really have Ivy or was it a bluff?

At the condo, Amos walked Buddy inside, flipped on the light, and turned to go. "I'll catch you later, Buddy. You gonna be all right?"

Buddy grabbed Amos's arm. "Hold on, I need you to do something for me."

"Liz is waitin' in the car. Whatta ya need?"

Buddy reached into his pocket and took out his wallet. Feeling inside, he pulled out a business card and handed it to Amos. "What does that say?"

"Says Detective John Allen, Memphis Police Department."

"There a phone number?"

"Yeah, there's a cell number written in pen across the front."

"Use my phone, call it."

"You sure? It's the middle of the night."

"Just dial it for me, then you can go."

"Something wrong?"

Buddy knew Amos must be torn between wanting to help him and the woman waiting in the car.

"Just need you to dial the phone, that's all."

"That what ya want." Amos walked across the room and a minute later, handed Buddy the phone receiver. After several rings, a sleepy voice answered.

"John Allen."

"Buddy O'Brian, John."

Amos touched Buddy on the shoulder and seconds later the door clicked shut behind him.

"Buddy," Allen was saying, "something wrong?"

"Sorry to call at this hour, but I need your help. How long before you can get here?"

"Actually, I'm on days off and I'm in Baton Rouge now. At Carolyn's."

A moment of guilt passed over Buddy. "Can you come over, John? I'll explain when you get here."

"Be there as soon as I can."

Allen hung up and the dial tone buzzed in Buddy's ear. He punched the speed dial for Jan's number, hoping Ivy would answer and the whole thing would be a big farce. But Jan's phone rang and rang until a machine picked up. He tried Ivy's cell but it went straight to voice mail. He slumped down in a chair and waited.

Chapter Thirty-Nine

Ivy was calm now, past the panic that had seized her when she realized she was being abducted. The three men weren't going to rape her, she decided. In fact, they didn't seem interested in her at all. They drove her to this seedy motel in Spanish town, shoved her inside a room and told her to sit down and shut up. Instead of the attack she thought was imminent, they laughed, gave each other high-fives and turned their backs to her.

"What do you want?" Ivy asked. "Why am I here?"

"Shut yo goddamn mouth ho," one said, "else I'll stuff a rag in it."

They left her with one man in the motel room.

"Just keep the bitch here, Tyrone. Don't talk to her or nuttin'. Be back in a couple of hours."

Tyrone watched television, sitting on one of the twin beds and leaning back against the wall; pillows propped behind his head, and with his dirty running shoes propped up on the faded spread. He was younger than the other two. Ivy guess he was still a teen-ager, maybe seventeen. His hair was in dreadlocks that felt to his shoulders. In the early morning hours, he watched an endless parade of old television series from the 1960s and 70s. The sitcoms and westerns flickered on the screen while he drank from a giant bottle of cola and munched on corn chips. Stuffed in the waistband of his low-riding jeans was a snub-nose thirty-two revolver. He lit up a joint and the sweet smell of pot caused Ivy to doze on the second bed, her sleep shallow and troubled.

She woke with a start when there was a pounding on the door and two men came in bringing a bag of MacDonald's biscuits with eggs. She took the coffee they handed her, wondering why they were keeping her, afraid to ask. They paid no attention to her, but settled into the room like mites in a carpet.

The men, two black and one white, dressed in jeans and tee-shirts with heavy metal band logos printed on front. The white guy wore a ball cap on backward and the third had a red bandanna tied around his forehead. Ivy remembered that Rufus used to wear a red bandanna when he played the drums. The two were older than Tyrone, Ivy guessed in their middle twenties. They sat at the round table in the motel room, and began playing cards and drinking Southern Comfort like they had all the time in the world. Ivy sat on the bed; her feet tucked up, her back against the headboard, and watched. Her mind raced with possible escape plans as the minutes crawled.

One of them jumped up and slapped Tyrone upside the head with his open palm. "Tyrone, you a lyin' bastard! You ain't got no straight. Cain't you count?"

"Ow!" Tyrone put his arm up to shield his head from any further blows.

"Let him alone Luther. You know he ain't finished but the sixth grade." The third man, who seemed to be the leader, calmly picked up the cards and began reshuffling.

"You always 'scoozing him J.G." Luther protested, but he sat down and picked up the cards being dealt to him. "He best learn to play cards or sit over with the girl."

"You want some cards or you standin' pat?" J.G. held the deck in his hand and looked at Luther. A nine millimeter Smith and Weston automatic lay on the table close to J.G.'s right hand. He had sunglasses pushed up on his forehead over the bandanna and his eyes were hard as black diamonds.

"I needs two," Tyone said, tossing cards on the table. "You think he'll show?"

"He'll show." J.G. slid two cards off the deck to him. "Iffin' he wants his main squeeze back."

"What we gonna do with all that money?" Tyrone picked up the cards and squinted at the numbers.

Ivy was beginning to understand now. These must be the men that beat up Jimmy and tried to carjack Franklin and Buddy. Now they were asking Buddy for ransom. She was going to have to find her own way out of this or they would kill her for sure.

"We goin' down to Miami and have us a big ole time," Luther said. "Get us some Cuban girls and some blow. Stay high for a week."

"That right, J.G.?" Tyrone asked. "Can we take her car?"

"You need cards or not, Luther?" J.G. said.

"Naw, I'll stay with these."

"Let's see what you got then."

"I jes wanna see that much money," Tyrone said.

J.G might be the leader, but Tyrone was the weak link, Ivy thought. She would work on him.

"Oh, man. It ain't right, Luther wining again," Tyrone moaned as Luther scooped up the cards and money.

"Why don't you let me play," Ivy said. "I can help Tyrone."

Luther and Tyrone looked at her and then at J.G. who was leaning back in his chair, his hands on the table.

"You know how?"

"I sang in a lot of casinos around here." Ivy knew that was pretty lame, so she added, "I know how. I play with the guys in the band."

"You got any money?"

"Sure, I got some in my purse."

"That's mine now, bitch" J.G. said. "So you don't got any. But we'll let you play anyhow. Sit over there by Tyrone, help him count."

Tyrone was sitting on the foot of the bed since the only two chairs in the room were taken by J.G. and Luther. Ivy moved to the edge beside him and looked at his cards. Tyrone smiled at her like a child asking for help from a teacher, and for a moment, Ivy actually felt sorry for him.

"Get rid of these," she instructed him, tapping two cards.

Tyrone won the next hand laughing and whooping as he raked the money to him. J.G smiled.

"That ain't right," Luther said. "I ain't playin' against the two of them."

"Chill out, Luther." J.G. picked up the Southern Comfort and poured some in Luther's glass and put the bottle to his lips to take a deep pull. He tipped the bottle toward Ivy, asking if she wanted some.

"I like ice in mine," she said.

"Oh, the lady likes ice in hers," Luther mocked.

"Go down the hall and get some ice." J.G. pushed some money toward Luther. "Hit the snack machine too, I'm hungry."

"We ain't got time for all that. It's after eleven now," Luther protested. But one glance at J.G.'s hard stare made him shrug and take the money. He picked up the ice bucket and left the room.

J.G shuffled the cards. He pointed to the empty chair and said "Sit down."

Ivy moved off the bed and took Luther's seat while J.G. began to deal.

Chapter Forty

"You sure they got her?" John Allen said. It was five a.m. when he and Carolyn arrived at Buddy's place.

"Said they did and I can't get her on the phone," Buddy answered, trying to be patient, wanting to grab Allen by the shirt and yell, let's go.

"Can you make some coffee, Carolyn?" Allen asked. "Okay with you, Buddy?"

"Yeah, sure. You can find the coffee tin in the refrigerator."

What the hell, now they wanted to drink coffee. Buddy hadn't liked it that Carolyn had come along with John Allen, but he understood when the detective told him he had no real authority in Baton Rouge, but Carolyn did, so they needed her.

"You think it's the same three that tried to carjack you?" Allen asked.

"Pretty sure I recognized the voice," Buddy said, putting together the guy who wanted to break his hands and the one who said he was Rufus's cousin, asking if he wanted his girlfriend back. "I thought you had them in jail."

"They made bail," Allen said. "We had to kick them loose. J.G., Tyrone and Rufus were all cousins. Luther is a tagalong. "

"Now they have Ivy. It never ends."

"Look, these guys are not rocket scientists; they're small time hoods, drug dealers," Allen said. "They set this up in a motel and tell you ahead of time where they are. Not too bright."

"Sometimes," Carolyn said, sitting cups of coffee on the table, "they're the most dangerous."

"That's why we need a plan," Allen said, scraping the sugar bowl across the table and tapping a spoon on the rim of his cup.

167

"They want five hundred thousand. I can't get that much," Buddy said.

"Maybe we can put something else in the case," Carolyn said. "I did a year with the bomb squad when I first came on the PD. It was one of those quota things and none of the other women wanted it."

"So what're you sayin'?"

"I think I can get the makings and wire it."

"Ivy might get hurt," Buddy said.

"It'll be up to you to see that she doesn't," Carolyn replied. "And she won't if you follow my instructions. You got a guitar case we can use?"

"I got a couple," Buddy said. He heard Allen chuckle.

"Get one," Carolyn said, "we don't have that much time."

"You never cease to amaze me," Allen said with affection in his voice.

"You ain't seen nuthin' yet," Carolyn teased.

Buddy got up and found his way across the room to the front closet where he kept a Fender in a hard case. He opened it and pulled the guitar out, ran his hand across the bottom and turned it upside down to be sure it was empty. A couple of guitar picks fell to the floor.

"Here you go," he said. "Wire it up."

"You guys wait here," Carolyn instructed. "I'll go get the stuff to put this together. Might not be any stores open yet, but I'll see what we got down at the station."

"Need me to go along?" Allen asked.

"Better stay with Buddy. Right now he needs you more than I do."

After Carolyn left, the room was quiet. The two men sat drinking coffee until Buddy reached for the telephone and called Jan's number again. When the machine picked up, he disconnected and called Ivy's cell. It went to voice mail. He sat down and ran his fingers through his hair, frustration mounting. He called Jan's number again, holding onto hope that Ivy would answer. This time, the phone picked up and he heard Jan say, "Hello?"

Stunned after all the empty rings, he took a minute to speak. "Jan, its Buddy. Is Ivy there?'

"I just walked in the door. I've been on a flight to Paris. Her car's not here, but let me go in and see if she's in bed."

Buddy heard Jan's footsteps move across the floor. "No, she not here and the bed hasn't been slept in. Did she stay with you last night?"

"No. Is there anywhere else she could have stayed?"

"Can't answer that, but my first thought would be no. Have you talked to her at all? You trying to make up?"

He didn't want to tell Jan that some scumball drug dealer had her sister because of him, so he just said, "If she comes in, or you talk to her, will you ask her to call me right away?"

"Is something wrong?"

"Just ask her to call." Buddy hung up. He was convinced now that the men had her. The last glimmer of hope that it was a bluff went out.

"I'll make some breakfast," John said. "You got bacon and eggs?"

"I ain't hungry. You go ahead."

"I'll fix some for both of us. You need to eat."

Buddy listened to John move around the kitchen, opening cabinet and refrigerator doors. Soon there was the teasing aroma of bacon frying and the sizzle of eggs in grease. John whistled while he worked and it all seemed so normal and easy while Buddy's world lay in ruins and his mind in desperation. In the back of his thoughts, the power of Jack Daniels called to him, but he pushed it away.

He pictured Ivy with these men. She must be so scared. What would they have done to her by now? All the years she had been the strong one and now he felt helpless to defend her. She was in this mess because of him, just as Jimmy had been hurt because of him. Now, here he sat drinking coffee with bacon frying while some low-life scum held her captive. Was she depending on him to come for her? Would he let her down one more time?

He ate the food Allen put in front of him, just to have something to do while they waited for Carolyn to come back. It seemed like hours before she knocked at the door and Allen jumped up to let her in.

"I think I got everything," she said. "Had everything I needed at the station."

A paper bag rattled as she unloaded it, naming off the contents. "Wire, blasting cap, nine volt battery, blasting powder and this little baby is a triggering device we can set to go off when they hit the locks. I can put this together right here on the floor."

"You're not going to blow us all to hell, are you doll?" Allen said.

"Have a little faith. This will take a while, so let me get started."

"I'll make another pot of coffee," Allen said. "You want something to eat, Carolyn?"

"Couple slices of toast would be good," she said.

Buddy listened to their give and take and noticed the easy way between them. They were more than lovers; they were friends and colleagues. The same way it was with him and Ivy, where they understood what made the other one go because it was the same thing that made them get up in the morning. The way music was their medium, the world of cops and robbers was Carolyn and Allen's.

Their small talk was making Buddy crazy. He wanted to yell and pound the wall.

Carolyn's cell phone rang and she stopped work to answer. When she hung up, she said, "We sent a team out to the motel to look around and they collared Luther at the vending machine. They took a weapon off him and he says they got Ivy in a room there. He says the other two are armed also. I told our men to stay out of sight and wait for us before doing anything."

"Why can't we just go in and get her? We know where they are," Buddy said.

The detective shook his head. "She's their only leverage. Try to storm them; they're dumb enough to kill her for sure."

Chapter Forty-One

"You do Texas hold 'em?" J.G. held the deck in his left hand and looked at Ivy.

"Let's keep it simple for Tyrone," Ivy said. "How 'bout low ball?"

J.G. looked sideways at his cousin. "You do that Lil' Tyrone?"

"If she helps me, I cain." Tyrone looked at Ivy with soft, dark eyes, the lashes long and thick as a girl's.

He's so needy, like a lost child, Ivy thought. "Sure, I'll help you. The way it works, you just pick the lowest numbers."

"Where's Luther with the food?" J.G. grumbled. "Probably ran into some ho. Pull that curtain open a little bit so we can watch for the taxi."

"I'll git ya a clean glass, Ivy," Tyrone said, getting up to open the dingy blue drapes. "One's in the bathroom. Soon' he get back with ice you cain have a drink."

"Thank you Tyrone, that's sweet," Ivy said. The last thing she wanted was a drink with these guys.

"Yo gots such pretty hair, cain I touch it?" He stood over her, looking down.

"Knock it off, Tyrone," J.G. said, flipping cards toward them.

Ivy took the elastic band from her hair and shook it out so that it fell on her shoulders. "You can touch it if you want."

Tyrone's fingers moved slowly toward Ivy as if he were reaching for fire. He placed the flat of his hand on her hair and moved down, caressing it lightly. "So soft."

"Let's play some cards," J.G said. A look of affection crossed his eyes and flickered away. "Don't mess with the merchandise."

I might be merchandise to you, Ivy thought, but not to Tyrone.

"He doesn't mean any harm," she said. "Do you, Tyrone?"

"No mam. You is just so pretty, is all."

"You want her, my man, you can have her," J.G. stood up. "I'll go find Luther. Leave ya'll alone."

Maybe I've gone too far, Ivy thought, panic rising; revolted at the thought of having this boy forced on her.

"I—I," Tyrone stammered.

"You go ahead, I give her to you," J.G. said, like a father presenting a gift to a child. "Might be my turn when you done, you say it's worth it."

"Well, she is real pretty," Tyrone seemed to warm to the idea, "and I think she be liking me. You likes me, don't you Miss Ivy?"

Ivy felt as if she might throw up. "No Tyrone," she said, shaking her head, "Don't do this. It's not right."

Maybe, she thought, if J.G. leaves, I can get Tyrone to let me go.

"Hot damn, here he is!" J.G. grabbed the Smith and Weston up from the table and looked out the window as a yellow taxi pulled across the gravel driveway.

The two men moved to each side of the window, concealed by the drapes and out of sight to anyone looking in. J.G. motioned for Ivy to get down on the bed, but instead, she stepped further back into the room.

The taxi stopped in front of the door and the driver got out. He was a guy in need of a shave, wearing a baseball cap and an old shirt hanging over dirty jeans. Ivy recognized him at once. She felt an overwhelming relief knowing John Allen was here.

Allen opened the back door of the car and Buddy stepped out. He stood in the noon sun, wearing dark glasses without a hat and his hair curled around his ears where the gold loop caught the light. He was carrying a guitar case and he looked wonderful. He had come for her and she was not alone anymore.

Buddy put his hand in his jeans pocket and came out with some bills that he handed to Allen who then turned him in the direction of the motel door. Allen got back into the taxi and pulled away, the wheels spinning gravel as the car turned back toward the street.

My God! Ivy thought, he doesn't have Mojo with him. She was afraid for Buddy now. Without Mojo for protection, he seemed so vulnerable. She would have to do something.

"Go on out and bring him in here," J.G. said to Tyrone, motioning with the gun.

"Let me do it," Ivy said. "You stay in here so no one sees you."

J.G. turned, gave her a hard look and said, "Stay where you are, bitch. Any funny business and he's a dead boyfriend."

"Ivy!" Buddy called from outside the door, "Ivy, are you there?"

"We gonna kill 'em?" Tyrone's eyes were wide with excitement.

"Buddy!" Ivy yelled. "Run, they have guns!"

J.G. swung around and hit her across the face with the back of his hand so hard that she fell to the floor. She lay there, her ears ringing, the metallic taste of blood in her mouth, pain throbbing in her cheek.

"No, J.G., don't hurt her!" Tyrone said. "She ain't done nuthin'."

"Open the door," J.G. ordered.

Tyrone unlocked the door and pushed it open. "In here."

Buddy stepped inside the room and Tyrone reached for the guitar case. "You bring the money?"

Buddy pulled the case back. "Send Ivy out first."

J.G. laughed. "We could just off you and take it. Get on to the back of the room while we take a look. "

Ivy scrambled to her feet and moved to Buddy. "I'm here. I'm okay."

Buddy relaxed his grip on the case and Tyrone pulled it from him.

"Put it on the table," J.G. commanded.

"Lemme open it."

"Luther's suppose to be here with the car," J.G. said. "Where the hell is he?"

"Lemme open it. I jes want to see that much money!"

J.G. backed up to the table, the semiautomatic in his hand pointed at Buddy and Ivy. "I'll do it. Keep your gun on them."

Tyrone took the thirty-two from the waistband of his pants and held it in both hands, with his arms outstretched.

Buddy put his arm around Ivy and held her to him. She clung to him and watched as J.G. ran his free hand along the smooth line of the black leather case. He stuck the gun in his waistband and reached for both locks and flicked them open. At the click of the locks, Buddy threw Ivy to the floor, falling with her, shielding her with his body as they landed between the beds.

The blast was sudden and loud, flashing like fireworks as cards and money flew from the table, spewing across the room. Smoke filled the air and slowly evaporated, leaving a stunned silence before all hell broke loose with men shouting and kicking the door. Ivy saw J.G. lying unconscious, the gun still in his waistband. Tyrone was backed against the window, his face wild with surprise and fear. He was still holding the pistol with both hands and waving it in front of him.

"J.G.!" he called. "J.G.!"

Ivy crawled across the few feet to J.G. and took the gun from his body, clasping it, one hand over the other, to keep it steady in her shaking hands.

Tyrone watched her like a frightened child. He held the at arms length, turned toward the sounds at the door and fired.

From her position on the floor, Ivy leveled J.G.'s gun at Tyrone and pulled the trigger, the report like thunder in her ears. She pulled the trigger again, powerless to stop.

Glass shattered as bullets hit the window and the motel door was busted open, hanging splintered and broken from its hinges. A voice yelled "Baton Rouge Police! Drop your weapon!"

Tyrone grabbed his abdomen, the red blood soaking his shirt and hands. He looked at Ivy in disbelief and a question in his eyes as if she had betrayed him. His lips formed the words, but no sound came out.

Tyrone's body convulsed with each blow as the bullets found their mark. The gun fell from his hand and he slumped down on the dirty carpet.

Ivy was still on her knees, sobbing, when she felt John Allen kneel beside her. He put his hands on hers and pried her finger from the gun's trigger.

"It's okay," he crooned. "Let go, Ivy. Give me the gun. It's over now. You're safe."

He pulled her fingers away, one by one, until the gun fell in his hand.

Then Buddy was there, taking her in his arms. "Oh, baby," he said, "Thank God!"

They walked out into the hot midday sun. A breeze came up and ruffled Ivy's hair, blowing it across her face. Several police cars arrived and parked at every angle in the gravel driveway, their red lights flashing and dispatcher's voices droning on in monotone over the radios. Uniformed officers filled the area, motioning spectators away and stringing yellow crime scene tape along the entry. The wind made the tape wave and pull against its anchors. Ivy looked over and saw Luther sitting in the back seat of one of the cars, his head bowed in defeat. A door opened in one of the patrol cars and Mojo bounded out, running to Buddy, barking and rubbing against him. He reached down and touched the dog, telling him it was okay now.

An ambulance arrived and the police cleared a path while it backed toward the door of the room where Tyrone and J.G. lay on the floor. Paramedics jumped from the ambulance and disappeared inside. After a time, they came out, carrying J.G. loaded on a stretcher. The red bandanna and the sunglasses were missing and his eyes were closed. His wrists were in handcuffs and there were leg irons on his ankles. No one has to be afraid of him anymore, Ivy thought.

Carolyn offered her hand said, "Good job Ivy."

"Is he dead?" Ivy asked, looking at J.G.

"No. He'll be okay."

"Tyrone?"

"Yes, he's dead."

"I killed him."

"You did the right thing."

Ivy began to cry. Maybe it was from nerves, relief, exhaustion or sadness, she didn't know. But she could still see Tyrone's face with that question in his eyes after she shot him, as if he didn't understand. She knew she would always see it in her dreams and would relive this day over and over.

One of the paramedics came over and handed Ivy a soft cloth to clean her face.

"Nasty bruise on your cheek," he said. "I can take you and let the doctor have a look at it."

"I'll be fine," Ivy said. "I just want to go home now."

"I'll get a black and white to take you," Carolyn said. "We'll get your statement later."

"Come back with me, baby," Buddy said. "We belong together, we always have."

"Yes." Ivy smiled and pushed the hair from her face. "I can't leave you alone for a minute."

Buddy kissed the top of her head. "It's a rough road to Carnegie Hall, ain't it?"

Epilog

Buddy stood in the wings. The band was already on stage. He heard the rumble of voices from a large audience hush slowly into silence. At last, he thought.

Ivy whispered, "They're dimming the house lights."

Buddy adjusted the black porkpie hat and straightened his dark glasses. He wore a black leather sport coat and a black shirt open at the neck to show the religious medal of an Irish saint. He reached out and touched Ivy's hand.

"We're really here," he said. "Is Jimmy out there?"

"Yes darling. He's in the front row with Jan. The theater is packed."

"What does this place look like?"

"The stage is large. The floor is polished wood and the curtains are heavy blue velvet. It's like in the movies," Ivy said, "or on television when we were kids and Judy Garland performed here. Remember, we watched her sit on the edge of the stage and sing *Somewhere Over the Rainbow.*"

Yes, thought Buddy, that's where this dream began.

The announcer's voice was clear and crisp over the sound system. "Good evening ladies and gentlemen and welcome to Carnegie Hall. Tonight we are proud to welcome to our stage a group with both a single recording and a CD scoring number one on the music charts. Please put your hands together and show your appreciation for an icon of American blues music; Blind Buddy and Mojo's Blues Band."

The crowd thundered applause and Ivy said, "This is it. We've made it at last. They're standing up for you. Let's go."

Buddy walked between Mojo and Ivy. Her satin dress rustled with every step as she led him across the stage. When they stopped, Mojo dropped to the floor and Ivy took the Gibson from its stand and placed it in Buddy's hand. He caressed the guitar like the old friend it was and drew comfort from it. He reached forward and touched the microphone. The band waited; the applause faded.

Buddy swung the guitar strap around his neck and shoulder, but before he hit the first chord there was something he needed to do. He reached up and touched the gold loop in his ear. The smell of sandalwood and a curtain of black hair surrounded him. His mother's voice murmured in French, calling him her little cabbage, her love.

"I want to dedicate this evening, this performance, to my mother, the late Yvette O'Brian," he said into the microphone that carried his voice across the auditorium. "I know she is waltzing across the heavens tonight."

His voice softened as he added, "Dance, *ma cherie.*"

The audience was silent. He could feel them waiting. His mouth, never dry before, felt like the Sierra desert.

Carnegie Hall, he thought. I made it. This is where I belong.

He swallowed hard and licked his lips. Then he heard himself count off the downbeat; one, two, three, four…

He hit the opening cords of *Last Call* and the crowd cheered. The other two guitars, piano and drum joined him, pushing the song on. When he sang, his voice, hoarse with emotion, filled the auditorium.

Last call, it's the last call for me
Last call now baby, it's the last call for me
Guy behind the bar says last call
Clock on the wall says last call
The good-bye in your voice
Gives me no choice
It's my last call

Maybe, he thought. Maybe this time it is the last call for sleazy motels, shady desk clerks, and his old friend Jack Daniels. Maybe…